THE ADVENTURES

of

BUBBA JONES

TIME-TRAVELING THROUGH
GRAND CANYON NATIONAL PARK

The Adventures of Bubba Jones is a Registered Trademark ⓡ of Jeff Alt

Library of Congress Cataloging-in-Publication Data On File

Paperback ISBN: 9780825309274
Ebook: 9780825308116

For inquiries about volume orders, please contact:
Beaufort Books
27 West 20th Street, Suite 1102
New York, NY 10011

sales@beaufortbooks.com

Published in the United States by Beaufort Books
www.beaufortbooks.com

Distributed by Midpoint Trade Book, a division of Independent Publishers Group
www.midpointtrade.com
https://www.ipgbook.com/

Printed in the United States of America

Interior design by Jamie Kerry of Belle Étoile Studios, and Mark Karis
Cover design and illustrations by Hannah Tuohy

A NATIONAL PARK SERIES

THE ADVENTURES
of
BUBBA JONES

TIME-TRAVELING THROUGH GRAND CANYON NATIONAL PARK

BY JEFF ALT

WITH ILLUSTRATIONS BY HANNAH TUOHY

BEAUFORT BOOKS
NEW YORK

Disclaimer

The Adventures of Bubba Jones is a piece of fiction. All the characters in this book are purely fictional, but the historical and scientific facts about Grand Canyon National Park are true and accurate. The maps are not true to scale. To create this book, the author explored Grand Canyon National Park. He interviewed park experts, combed through museums and visitor centers, and cross-checked a wealth of park facts to verify accuracy, with sources listed in the bibliography.

Dedicated to Beth, Madison & William,
my adventurous family

ACKNOWLEDGEMENTS

I would like to thank the entire Beaufort Books publishing team, especially Eric Kampmann, my publisher, and his son Arthur for joining me on my Grand Canyon research adventure. I would like to thank Megan Trank, my managing editor, for assembling *The Adventures of Bubba Jones* into this book and getting it into the hands of those seeking an entertaining and informative adventure. I would also like to thank the following people who were instrumental in the publication of this book: Hannah Tuohy, my illustrator, for her talents in bringing my characters to life; Carly DaSilva for her editorial guidance; Bill Dietzer for his historical advice; Kendall Hauer, Ph.D, Director, Limper Geology Museum, Miami University, for his geology review of my manuscript; my daughter, Madison Alt, for assembling the discussion questions for this edition; I would like to thank the staff from Grand Canyon National Park for providing information and resources, reviewing my manuscript for accuracy, and providing advice, especially: Todd Stoeberl, Acting Chief of Interpretation and Resource Education; Eugenia Sullivan, Volunteer in Park Librarian & Edward "Ted" McClure, Librarian. I would like to thank Jennifer Wilcox, Museum Administrator &

Educational Coordinator, National Cryptologic Museum, National Security Agency, for advising me on a secret code appropriate for the young readers of this book series. And lastly, I would like to thank all of my family and friends that have explored our great National Parks with me over the years, which helped me develop this book.

CONTENTS

CHAPTER 1

WHITE WATER & MOLDY BACON

Our vessel moved swiftly down the Colorado River, snaking along in a westward direction, sandwiched between tall red walls of rock as far as the eye could see. The boat seemed pretty dangerous; it was made of wood and looked more like an antique you'd see in a museum rather than something you could safely ride through sudden bursts of life-threatening whitewater.

"Hang on, we're heading toward a series of rapids!" Papa Lewis shouted, as water crashed over boulders up ahead.

Our grandfather Papa Lewis, named after the famed Meriwether Lewis of the Lewis and Clark expedition, had explored Grand Canyon National Park on many adventures and had shared all his exciting stories with us. I'd always thought a park with "Grand" in its name must be spectacular, and I was right! Grand Canyon is one of the seven natural wonders of the world, and was designated as a forest reserve in 1893. Then it was declared a national monument in 1908, and it finally became a national park on February 26, 1919. Whenever Papa Lewis told us about Grand Canyon National Park (consistently ranked as the second most visited park in the U.S.), he always smiled, but it was always a serious kind of smile. The fact that he smiled at all meant this park was fun, but the seriousness of it meant the Grand Canyon was also full of unpredictable, dangerous, and exciting adventures.

Papa Lewis explained to us before our trip that most people experience Grand Canyon from the top rim. The South Rim attracts the bulk of visitors, a smaller number of people view Grand Canyon from the North Rim, and a much smaller number of people explore Grand Canyon below the rim. Even though our home had plenty of Grand Canyon books with stunning pictures, they didn't compare at all to seeing everything with our own eyes. The canyon ranges from 4,000 to 6,000 feet deep, so when you peer down into it you're seeing approximately one whole mile down! Its widest point is 18 miles across from rim to rim and it's 277 miles long, encompassing a total of 1,217,403 acres. Papa Lewis told us he wanted to introduce us to Grand Canyon

"Major-John-Wesley-Powell style."

We had no idea what that could mean!

But based on the fact that we were floating down the Colorado River, I was pretty sure we were part of the smaller number of visitors that explore Grand Canyon below the rim, and we were about to find out.

As if to confirm this, our boat suddenly began bobbing and bouncing in every direction, and we were showered with a constant mist of bone-chilling water. We all wore clothes that didn't have the wicking ability of my usual layered synthetic, waterproof, and breathable adventure wear; I had on a long-sleeved cotton shirt, scratchy wool pants held up by suspenders, a wool suit jacket, a bow tie, and a brimmed hat. Papa Lewis and my dad, Clark, wore the same. My sister Jenny (affectionally nicknamed "Hug-a-Bug" for her love of everything outdoorsy) wore an ankle-length dress and a bonnet. We seemed to be dressed more for a church service in the late 1800s rather than for a rafting trip down one of the most dangerous rivers in the U.S.

You might be wondering why that is, why my family and I thought taking a rickety boat downriver in these outfits was a good idea in the first place! Well, if you've followed us on some of our other national park adventures, then you already know our secret. But if you haven't, here it is: I can time travel (and soon, Hug-a-Bug will be able to do it, too)!

My sister and I inherited this amazing skill from Papa Lewis. Our family's legendary time travel skill goes all the way back to the time of the Lewis and Clark expedition. When Meriwether Lewis and William Clark returned from their Corps of Discovery expedition, our ancestors realized that the pristine wildlands Lewis and Clark explored were at risk of obliteration without careful preservation. Many people would soon head west. New cities and towns would take root and the untouched wilderness that Lewis and Clark explored could soon be gone forever. Our ancestors made it their mission to use time travel to help conserve and protect wilderness areas so that future generations could enjoy them. Not only that, but they hoped that their efforts would help preserve as much of the natural world as possible.

So, our ancestors dispersed throughout the U.S. over many lifetimes, protecting Mother Nature in all her glory as much as they could for future generations. This all happened long before the creation of the National Park Service and National Forest Service.

Our family's time travel skills came with a strict set of rules. The ability must be passed on to the next of kin every forty years. It must skip a generation and be given to a family member who not only can explore America's wildlands, but is willing to inherit both the magic itself and the responsibility that comes with it. Hug-a-Bug and I agreed to accept this skill from our Papa Lewis, of course. How could we refuse? Going back and seeing history happen is amazing, way better than learning about it in history class!

Our boat and our clothes would fit right in if anyone

saw us at that moment, but they made staying alive on the river as difficult for us as it was for anyone else in the late 1800s!

A wall of white water loomed over us, then crashed down into our boat, completely soaking every inch of my body. Wave after wave ferociously slammed us with such powerful force that everyone had to cling to the safety rope handles Papa Lewis instructed us to hold onto to keep us from falling overboard. Our boat was suddenly like a bathtub full of water! I was completely drenched and so cold it was hard to breathe. We wouldn't be able to keep this up much longer; our boat would surely soon fill with water and sink.

My fear overtook me. I could hear my heartbeat loud in my ears.

"Bubba Jones, *paddle!*" Papa Lewis shouted.

My real name is Tommy, but everyone calls me Bubba Jones. I guess you could say, Bubba Jones is my adventure name; similar to long distance hikers who take on a trail name or a boater who names his boat.

I snapped out of my cold trance and dipped my paddle into the water. Our boat had turned sideways and Papa Lewis was working hard to try to straighten us out and get the bow to point downriver again. I paddled like he told me, and it seemed like maybe we'd both be able to get us on course.

But all of a sudden we jerked to a stop and heard the distinctive sound of wood against rock. We were all flung forward like mannequins in a seatbelt safety commercial.

I looked over my shoulder and immediately saw the source of the sound: a boulder had caught on the left side of our boat, tearing a deep gash into the wood.

Papa Lewis placed his hands onto the boulder and pushed with all his might. I moved to help him, but his strength was thankfully enough; the boat was dislodged! We all scrambled for our oars and paddled in sequence, guided by Papa Lewis's coaching and our fear of drowning. Eventually, to our relief, the water calmed and the thrashing waves stopped. Everyone sat quietly for a moment after that, coming down from the adrenaline rush.

"Well, that was interesting," Papa Lewis muttered to himself, waist-deep in water, his paddle in hand.

"I think 'dangerous' is a better adjective!" said Hug-a-Bug.

That was just the first of a series of rapids on our route and we had already sustained damage to our vessel. Wooden crates labeled 'food supplies' floated by. Further upriver, I could see more wooden boats like ours and based on the many items bobbing about in the water, they had lost some of their supplies and took damage, too.

A commanding male voice could be heard from a distance: "We still have flour, dried apples, spoiled bacon, and a sack of coffee!"

"Yep, that's Major John Wesley Powell up ahead with his crew. The food items he mentioned are officially documented in his book chronicling this expedition," Papa Lewis confirmed as he pulled an antique brass telescope away from his eye and handed it to me to look through.

I held the telescope up and focused on the boats off in the distance. The view was amazing! I saw a man who was missing his right arm; he gestured with his left as he stood up in his boat.

"The man with one arm is Major John Wesley Powell," Papa Lewis explained as I continued to peer through the telescope.

Major John Wesley Powell was surrounded by a crew of men who sat in three boats tied together. It was apparent that he was their leader. Some of his crew appeared to argue with him despite this, as they bailed water out of their boats with buckets. If I had to guess what they were arguing about, I would think it had something to do with the danger of continuing their journey.

I passed the telescope to Hug-a-Bug so she could have a look. She studied the scene and then passed the telescope along to our dad for a peek.

"Let's stop at that beachhead over there to get some distance between us and Major John Wesley Powell's expedition so we aren't seen. We don't want to draw any attention!" Papa Lewis pointed to a small narrow sand beach along a high canyon wall. We paddled our boat close to the shore, then Dad hopped into the water and guided it along with a rope until it was up on the sand and safely out of the water. Everyone hopped out, and I picked up a floating bucket, mimicking what I saw Major Powell's crew doing to get as much water out of the boat as possible.

"These people are risking their lives going down the

Colorado River in these wooden boats, especially without life vests! Why would Major John Wesley Powell continue?" I asked Papa Lewis. "He already lost supplies, and he has to know by now that his boats aren't made for the rough white water."

"Bubba Jones, you're right," Papa Lewis agreed. "Navigating the Colorado River through Grand Canyon is very dangerous under these circumstances. So, let's try to understand why Major John Wesley Powell would attempt this journey."

"After Lewis and Clark reached the west coast in 1806, Grand Canyon was considered one of the last unexplored areas in the U.S., though indigenous peoples called it home long before this. Grand Canyon appeared as part of a big blank area on maps that was referred to as 'The Great Unknown.' The first Europeans to see Grand Canyon were part of a Spanish expedition led by García López de Cárdenas in 1540, but they didn't explore much below the rim, or the Colorado River for that matter."

"In 1857 an Army officer, First Lieutenant Joseph Christmas Ives, attempted to head up the Colorado River from the Gulf of California on a steamboat, but his vessel could not hold up to the ferocious river and it crashed before he could make it to the canyon. He continued with a smaller boat after that, and eventually had to resort to foot travel. He managed to make it to the canyon on foot, but that's as far as he got. He became the first European American to reach the Grand Canyon part of the Colorado River. Even so, Grand Canyon remained largely unknown to most U.S. Americans until Major John Wesley Powell's expedition in 1869.

"Major John Wesley Powell wanted to make a name for himself as an explorer of the west. He was a wounded hero from the Civil War who'd lost his arm in battle, but that didn't stop him from pursuing an adventurous life! He set out to discover the canyons of the Green, Grand, and Colorado River. Major Powell personally designed these boats for his expedition. He started out with four boats and ten men, but one boat cracked in half after it hit a rock and one man quit the expedition less than a month into the journey before they reached the confluence of the Grand and Green Rivers. As you can see, provisions went overboard as they struggled to navigate the treacherous waters. They survived on moldy bacon, dried apples, rotten flour, and coffee. They had rifles to hunt with, but there wasn't any wild game worth hunting along the deep canyon."

"A few days before Major John Wesley Powell successfully made it through, three more of his men decided to quit. Morale was low and even the crew that stayed with Major Powell didn't think they would make it out alive. The three men that quit decided that they had a better chance of survival on foot. They climbed out of Grand Canyon and were never heard from again. What happened to them remains a mystery. But just two days after they left, Major Powell reached the end of Grand Canyon with just two remaining boats. He returned to navigate the Colorado River through Grand Canyon and completed a second expedition in 1872. On this expedition, he had better equipment to record and document his journey. After that, Grand Canyon no longer remained a blank spot on maps."

"So, Major John Wesley Powell took all that risk for the sake of an adventure, okay, that's great. Can we skip out on the rest of his journey, please?" Hug-a-Bug asked. "Moldy bacon and rotten flour sounds disgusting."

"Agreed, Hug-a-Bug!" Papa Lewis laughed. "We'll finish our Colorado River adventure Papa-Lewis style."

CHAPTER 2

DROPPING BY IN THE MOST UNUSUAL WAY

By the way, I need to let you in on another little secret. We were here exploring Grand Canyon for more than just a vacation; this adventure was actually a special assignment!

When I inherited my time travel skills from Papa Lewis in the Great Smoky Mountains, we used our family magic to solve a mystery there. Word of our success quickly got out to our family network in other national parks, and they immediately began requesting our assistance. This was now our fourth official national park assignment.

We received a secret coded message requesting urgent help from our Arizona relatives.

KBBA	VLRO	EBIM	FK	DOXKA	ZXKVLK
XOOFSB	JXGLO	MLTBII	PQVIC		

With our family's magical abilities comes the risk that someone with bad intentions could try to take advantage of them for mischievous purposes. So, we communicate like spies as a precaution to keep our secret from falling into the wrong hands! Our Arizona kin's mission is to help protect and preserve the wildlands in the Grand Canyon region. They also serve as keepers of our family secret. Various branches of our family have different roles and capabilities, and when we received the message, we weren't sure what their emergency was or what their magical abilities could be. We managed to figure out what the message said with this cipher here!

Plain:	NEED	YOUR	HELP	IN	GRAND	CANYON
Cipher:	KBBA	VLRO	EBIM	FK	DOXKA	ZXKVLK

Plain:	ARRIVE	MAJOR	POWELL	STYLE
Cipher:	XOOFSB	JXGLO	MLTBII	PQVIC

Plain	A	B	C	D	E	F	G	H	I	J	K	L	M
Cipher	X	Y	Z	A	B	C	D	E	F	G	H	I	J

Plain	N	O	P	Q	R	S	T	U	V	W	X	Y	Z
Cipher	K	L	M	N	O	P	Q	R	S	T	U	V	W

The decoded message also said that we would be approached by someone and gave us the passwords to use so we could authenticate our identities. The messenger would greet us with the password "bighorn." We would then respond by saying, "Jupiter."

We arrived in the Grand Canyon region late at night. Early the next morning, before we experienced Major John Wesley Powell's legendary expedition, we enjoyed the peaceful beauty of the rising morning sun as we rambled along a gravel road in our four-wheel drive. Mom and Grandma Lewis dropped us off at the edge of the Colorado River on the Hualapai (pronounced "wall-a-pie") Reservation. The Hualapai are one of eleven tribes indigenous to the United States with historical ties to Grand Canyon. We planned to link back up with Mom and Grandma Lewis at our rendezvous point, another fifty miles downriver, at the end of the day.

The river buzzed with activity. Trucks with boat trailers were parked near its banks, and raft guides were busy preparing tourists eager to start their whitewater adventure. Papa Lewis spoke to a man who then led us to one of the many pontoon rafts along the shoreline. There were several rafting options: half-day, full-day, or multiple days. We chose an elite full-day excursion that Papa Lewis worked out for us in advance with him as our official river guide. Shortly after we hopped in our raft and floated far enough from onlookers, Papa Lewis instructed me to take us back to Major John Wesley Powell's Grand Canyon Expedition in 1869. We were near the historic Separation Canyon, which got its name from the three explorers who left Major Powell's expedition on foot and were never seen or heard from again.

My time travel magic is linked to our family journal, a leather-bound pocket notebook that Papa Lewis carried with him for forty years and then handed down to me. The journal dates all the way back to the Lewis and Clark expedition! When I hold it, everyone within ten feet of me can travel into the past and return to the present along with me. Whenever we go back in time, our clothing and personal effects magically change to fit the period. All morning, we had traveled along the Colorado River in 1869, secretly following Major John Welsey Powell as directed. Now, we huddled together on the narrow, sandy beach along the bank of the Colorado River, soaked through after just barely making it through those rapids.

"Bubba Jones, we should probably head back to the present while no one is looking and before Major John Wesley Powell takes notice of us," Papa Lewis suggested.

When we time travel, we're supposed to blend in as much as possible and not disrupt anything or risk altering the future. "Take us back to the present!" I declared.

Everything went dark and a vacuum force tugged my entire body. Then, there was light. I blinked my eyes a few times and peered around.

We were still huddled on the sandy beach, but our

clothes were modern again. Hug-a-Bug, Dad, and I were back in our wicking synthetic t-shirts and khaki zip-off pants, and I had my baseball cap on like usual. Papa Lewis wore his signature vintage World War II khaki pants with cargo pockets, a shirt with its long sleeves rolled up to the elbows, and a wide-brimmed hat. His long grey beard really made him look like a seasoned mountain man, and his glasses added an intellectual flair. Thankfully, we now all wore our life vests. Our boat was back to being a large inflatable raft. It was pulled halfway out of the water; the back half bobbed with the waves. This was a much safer way to explore the Colorado River for sure.

From off in the distance, a kayaker began to paddle toward our little beach. They wore a safety helmet and a life vest and they navigated the rapids we had just barely made it through as if they were no trouble at all. As the kayak grew near, the stranger's bearded face looked vaguely familiar, and then a familiar voice rang out. "Well, I finally caught up to you guys!"

It was Wild Bill, Papa Lewis's cousin! We tracked him down in the Great Smoky Mountains as part of our first national park mystery.

"What are you doing out here, Bill?" Papa Lewis asked with some excitement in his voice.

"I heard you might need some help on this mission, Lewis. Word travels fast through our time travel family, especially with the reputation you all have earned solving park mysteries, and I love Grand Canyon. I heard this was an urgent emergency, so I'm offering my support," Wild Bill explained.

"Glad to have you on board, Bill," Papa Lewis crowed as he pulled Wild Bill's kayak up onto the sand.

"Wow, Wild Bill, you handled those rapids like a pro!" Hug-a-Bug exclaimed.

"Thanks, Hug-a-Bug! I love the thrill of white water and I must say, these high narrow fluted rock columns we've been passing by are pretty cool," Wild Bill replied.

"These fluted rock formations were created by erosion, mostly from water. Before Glen Canyon Dam was built, the Colorado would sweep through with tons of sediments that would scrape the rocks, especially during the spring flood with sediments sometimes as large as houses," Papa Lewis explained.

"How did you find us out here?" I asked Wild Bill.

"Your Papa Lewis alerted me of your plans and left his itinerary with me in case of an emergency. I thought I would do one better and join you myself."

Papa Lewis always taught us to leave our adventure plans with someone we trust in case something goes wrong, and he practices what he preaches. After conversing with Wild Bill for a few minutes, we all slipped back into our raft and continued a much easier trip downriver. Wild Bill followed us in his kayak. Whitewater is universally classified on a scale of one to six, one being the easiest and six being the most dangerous and difficult. Grand Canyon had its own classification, but most of the river guides now use and refer to the universal system.

We splashed swiftly along through several Class II-IV rapids before reaching our rendezvous point further down river: Pearce Ferry Ramp. We were now outside the boundary of Grand Canyon National Park. Our inflatable raft handled the rapids way better than those old rickety wooden vessels that Major John Wesley Powell used. As we neared the shore, Dad and Papa Lewis hopped into the river near the bank and pulled our raft up onto land. Several other groups were on the shore loading their rafts onto trailers hitched to trucks and piling gear into vans and buses after completing their journey. Like clockwork, Mom and Grandma Lewis stood near our four-wheel-drive, waving to get our attention. We waved back and they walked up to greet us. Mom and Grandma were confused when they saw Wild Bill so we had to explain how he caught up with us on the river. They had not seen him since our Smoky Mountain adventure.

Suddenly our conversations were muffled by a choppy, repetitive thudding sound mixed with the roar of a high-powered motor. A helicopter hovered overhead and then dropped down onto a nearby clearing, kicking sand up into the air. The engine powered down and the rotor blades slowed but continued to spin. The side door sprung open and the pilot stepped out, looking directly at us.

"Papa Lewis, do you know that guy?" I asked.

"I'll let you know if I do," Papa Lewis replied cautiously.

The pilot walked past the other rafters and strolled right up to us. He stopped a few feet away. His flight helmet had a dark eye visor which made it difficult to identify who he was. He wore a pilot jumpsuit speckled with aviation patches; there was a U.S. flag patch on his shoulder.

"Bighorn," the pilot said.

It was the messenger! He *literally* dropped by, like, out of the *sky* dropped by, and he had spoken the secret word!

"Jupiter!" I immediately responded.

CHAPTER 3

MISSION IN THE SKY

"Bubba Jones, Hug-a-Bug, Lewis, and Clark, I presume?" the pilot asked, grinning.

"That's us, and this is also Wild Bill, my mom, and Grandma Lewis," I replied. "Who are you?"

"I'll explain later. Right now, I need to get you all airborne fast. This isn't technically a landing area; I had to get special permission to land the chopper here."

"We have Wild Bill's kayak and that vehicle over there," Papa Lewis said, pointing over at the kayak strapped to the top of the four-wheel drive. "And we probably have more people than will fit in your helicopter."

"Yeah, anyone who doesn't fly with me will have to take the car. But I'd like to have the famous mystery sleuths come along with me so I can get them up to speed on the situation."

"That would be Bubba Jones and Hug-a-Bug here." Papa Lewis put a hand on each of our shoulders. "I'll fly along, too."

"Where are we going?" I asked.

"Williams, Arizona. But that could change as things develop," the pilot answered.

Wild Bill looked up from his map with a smile. "This route here will take us along a stretch of historic Route 66. I've always wanted to cruise Route 66."

"We'll keep in touch with our cell or satellite phones, okay Clark?" Papa Lewis turned to his son and clapped him on the back.

"Gotcha, Pops," Dad replied as he jumped into the passenger seat of the four-wheel drive. Mom hopped into the driver's seat. Wild Bill and Grandma Lewis got in the back and with that, their vehicle began snaking away up a gravel road, leaving a trail of dust behind.

Hug-a-Bug, Papa Lewis, and I followed the pilot to the helicopter. There were a lot of firsts for Hug-a-Bug and me on this adventure already, and we had only been here *one* day! I had visited Grand Canyon for the first time, rafted the Colorado River for the first time, and now I was about to take my first ever helicopter ride. I was so excited!

We climbed into the helicopter, buckled up, and put

our helmets on. The pilot reviewed the chopper's safety rules with us and pointed out where the first aid kit and emergency equipment were located. Then he powered up the engine and we lifted off nice and slow, like a spider climbing up a web to the sky. The ground grew smaller, and the Colorado River looked like a bold reddish brown line from up high, nothing like the wide river we'd just rafted. Then, we cleared Grand Canyon's walls, and I was stunned. This was my first in-person overhead view of Grand Canyon and it was way beyond what I expected!

The canyon walls are made of red, grey, tan, and black rough-edged rock layers stacked on top of each other. They were closest together at the river's edge, and they fanned out all the way up to the top and were farthest apart at the rim. It was easy to recognize from this perspective how the Colorado River had carved out Grand Canyon very slowly over time. As I drank in the sight of it all, I realized why Grand Canyon is one of the seven natural wonders of the world.

"Amazing view, isn't it?" the pilot said. He didn't have to shout over the helicopter's noise thanks to a mic and speakers in our helmets.

"It sure is," Papa Lewis agreed.

"Grand Canyon is 5.7 million years old," the pilot added.

"It's so beautiful!" Hug-a-Bug exclaimed.

"This is awesome," I said as I continued to gawk at the view.

"It never gets old, seeing it from up here." The pilot

sighed. "This is my own personal helicopter. I also fly patrols and search and rescue missions for the National Park Service."

Our flight continued along Grand Canyon's rim for several minutes before we veered south and away from it.

"Alright, we're headed towards Williams!" The pilot's voice crackled through our helmet speakers.

"What's in Williams, and how can we help you?" I asked. "You haven't told us yet."

"Lewis, do you remember how to fly this thing? Can you take the controls?"

"You bet, T2," Papa Lewis replied. I realized then that he and the pilot must know each other from somewhere. I had no idea Papa Lewis could fly helicopters, but then again, my grandpa is the guy that had magic powers and decided to pass them on to me, so I shouldn't have been so surprised that he could fly, too.

The helicopter had dual flight controls for a left- or right-seated pilot. Papa Lewis sat in the right front seat and immediately took control of the aircraft. Now that Papa Lewis was piloting, T2 turned around and faced Hug-a-Bug and me in the back seats. He flipped his visor up and showed us his face. He definitely looked like he could be a relative of ours; his facial features resembled both Dad's and Papa Lewis's except he had a deep bronze tan. His sharp eyes and stone-cold grin let us know that whatever he was going to tell us, it was going to be serious.

"You can call me T2," he began. "I'm the one that

requested your help. We've heard about your success with our relatives in other national parks and I hope you can help us out here, 'cause we've got a serious problem. As you know, we're your relatives that have helped preserve and protect the Grand Canyon region since the time of the Lewis and Clark expedition. What you probably don't know is that we were also tasked with protecting a closely guarded family tool. This tool is both powerful and magical, and if it ever got into the wrong hands, it could alter the world we live in forever. I discovered it was missing a few days ago. That was when I reached out to you."

"What's the magic tool that's missing?" I asked T2.

"It's a time travel lens. It was part of this telescope." As he spoke, T2 reached over and placed the cylindrical body of the telescope in my hands. It looked just like the one we used when we'd rafted behind Powell's expedition, but the magnifying lens was missing. It looked like the seal or whatever had held the lens in place was gone as well.

"This telescope has been in our family's possession for 150 years. We only use it to time travel. When we expand the telescope look through it, and request a specific date or precise time, we're sent to that time period. But now the lens is missing, and the telescope's time travel capability doesn't work," T2 explained.

"Who else knows about the magic of this telescope?" Hug-a-Bug asked.

"The only living people that know about it are my wife, Sydney, and our two adopted children, Blaze and Song. That's why we're headed to Williams. Our kids left on a Grand Canyon adventure organized by their school's Adventure Club and that's when we noticed the lens was missing. The club's adventure started at Williams Railway Depot. The entire Adventure Club group rode into Grand Canyon National Park by train. We want to retrace our kids' routes to make sure we don't miss any place it could be. My wife is waiting for us at Grand Canyon National Park Airport. From there, we will drive to the train depot in Williams," T2 replied.

"So, why did you tell us to raft the Colorado River Major John Wesley Powell style in your cipher?" I asked him.

"According to family legend, this telescope was used on Major John Wesley Powell's expedition and we believe the magical lens inside the telescope dates to the Lewis and Clark expedition. I thought you might pick up a clue if you started your adventure at the origin of the telescope. Lewis and I rafted that section of the Colorado River and I knew he would know where to go." T2 put his visor down, turned back around to face forward, and took control of the helicopter from Papa Lewis. I thought back to our rafting trip, trying to remember as much as I possibly could.

When we followed Major John Wesley Powell, Papa Lewis used the same kind of telescope as the one T2 had just handed me. When I looked through Papa Lewis's, it worked just as a telescope should. I didn't recall anything special about it.

Our helicopter hovered over an airport and then

descended towards a helipad. In seconds we were safely on the ground and T2 powered down the motor. We removed our helmets, opened our doors, and stepped out onto the tarmac, ducking down and clinging to our hats. A dark-haired woman wearing a turquoise necklace stood next to an SUV and waved at us as we approached her, led by T2.

"This is my wife, Sydney," he introduced. "Sydney, this is Bubba Jones, Hug-a-Bug, and do you remember Lewis from our adventure on the Colorado River many years ago?"

"How could I ever forget Lewis," Sydney said as she hugged Papa Lewis. She then turned to Hug-a-Bug and me. "Nice to meet you kids. Thanks for coming out on such short notice."

"I hope we can help," I told her, and she smiled.

"Climb on in, all of you. We should be on our way."

We climbed into the SUV, Sydney sliding into the driver's seat, and once we were all buckled up, she drove us out of the airport and off to the Williams Train Depot. She talked while she drove, looking at Hug-a-Bug and me every so often through the car's rearview mirror.

"Bubba Jones and Hug-a-Bug," she began, "with your parents' permission, we would like for you to accept a special assignment. We want you to join Blaze and Song on their Adventure Club's Grand Canyon trip. If your parents approve, I will have you both enrolled in the club as visiting students and you will join the school trip that's already in progress.

"T2 and I adopted Blaze and Song last year. They were my brother's kids, twins. He and his wife died a few years ago in a terrible accident. We've known Blaze and Song since birth and were happy to take them in." Sydney shared a long look with T2, and it was easy to see that they cared very much about their niece and nephew, now their own children. "My brother and I were twins just like Blaze and Song are, and we're Navajo on my father's side. Though I don't live on the Navajo reservation myself, I have family there, and my brother was always eager for his children to know their heritage, as am I. So, we often bring them there to spend time with my big extended family.

"My brother had passed away without ever learning T2's family time travel secret, and now, Blaze and Song are ours, destined to be inheritors of this knowledge. At first, we didn't share our family mission and secret with them; we weren't really sure how to go about doing it."

"But one day, while we were all on an adventure in the park, I decided to show them the magic telescope and I took them back in time," T2 chimed in. "I told them all about our family mission and its secret. I explained that they could one day take this mission on themselves and be the keepers of our magic telescope. I taught them some of our codes and ciphers and the other methods we use to communicate and keep our magic safe from others." He paused a moment, then continued. "Blaze and Song had the telescope with them through all of this. They were the last to have it when I knew the telescope definitely had its working lens. It was after that adventure that I noticed the lens was missing."

"But they wouldn't take it! There's no way they took it," Hug-a-Bug insisted, and Sydney nodded.

"I don't think they took it either, Hug-a-Bug. They seemed amazed and excited by the news, and they've never been the type of kids to make trouble. The lens could have fallen out, or they could have removed it by accident."

"Or maybe they did remove the lens because they wanted to have more fun learning about the past through time travel," T2 proposed. "They don't fully understand all the magic lens's rules and limits. We do need to find that lens and keep it out of the wrong hands, but more importantly, we just want to make sure that Blaze and Song are safe and that they don't misuse the time travel power and end up hurting themselves or others by accident. This is where you two come in. Your mission is to locate the lens and keep it from being used in the wrong way or falling into dangerous hands. Do you accept the mission?"

I looked over at Hug-a-Bug for approval. She smiled and nodded yes to me. "Sounds like fun," she commented, and I could tell she was excited to meet Blaze and Song and hopefully become their friend as well as their relative.

"My sister and I accept the mission," I declared.

"What happened to their parents?" Hug-a-Bug asked.

"They were killed in a car accident. The driver of the car that hit them was texting and driving. His car swerved into incoming traffic and hit their van," Sydney recounted, her voice solemn.

"That's so sad. It makes me so mad that people forget about safety for a dumb text message," Hug-a-Bug muttered.

"It makes me mad, too," T2 replied. "Well, thanks for agreeing to the mission. We'll be with you every step of the way. You can abort at any time, of course. Your Papa Lewis, your parents, and Wild Bill can tail you guys and meet up with you along the way. We will need to keep out of sight though. The adventure camp is supervised and planned by experienced guides, teachers, and counselors who probably wouldn't like a bunch of parents following them around too closely."

"Where do they go to school?" Hug-a-Bug asked.

"They go to Grand Canyon School which is part of the Grand Canyon Unified School District, and it's the only public school in the country that is actually *in* a national park. Since T2 works for the park, a perk is that they get to go to school in the park," Sydney clarified.

"Wow, Grand Canyon National Park has a school? You can go to school smack dab in the middle of a national park? That's so cool!" I exclaimed.

"This is a big national park, but it's located far away from other towns and cities, so it serves as a community for the local people as well as a tourist destination. Grand Canyon National Park has its own bank, community library, clinic, post office, grocery store, and water supply, too," T2 added.

We pulled into the parking lot near the train depot and met up with Mom, Dad, Grandma Lewis, and Wild

Bill, making sure to introduce them formally to T2 and Sydney and brief them on the mission. Mom and Dad told Hug-a-Bug and I that they would approve of our mission as long as we were comfortable with the plan, which we were. Sydney is a member of the school's parent–teacher association. She helps with community-based activities for the school, and after she made a few phone calls and had our parents sign a couple of digitally delivered documents, Hug-a-Bug and I were enrolled as visiting students in the Grand Canyon Adventure Camp. The counselors in charge of the trip were alerted that two newly enrolled students would arrive by train tomorrow morning and join their group for the remainder of the trip. The plan was taking shape. We just needed to make sure we kept our cover.

CHAPTER 4

TRAINS & PRESIDENTS

"The Railway runs two trains a day into the park, and both already left the station today, so I bought tickets for the 9:30 am train tomorrow. Sydney and I booked everyone hotel rooms right here across the street from the depot, so it'll be easy to get here in the morning," T2 explained.

We checked into our rooms, and then Mom and Grandma Lewis wheeled in a cooler and broke out an assembly line of deli meats, bread, cheese, lettuce, tomato, baby carrots, and drinks for dinner. After we ate, I could barely keep my eyes open I was so exhausted! We had covered a lot of ground (and water) in one day. I fell asleep as soon as my head hit the pillow and I didn't move until my alarm's buzzing woke me up at 7:30 am.

Everyone met up for breakfast at the hotel restaurant, and once we had our fill we checked out of our rooms and gathered in front of the train station. Wild Bill decided the night before that he wanted to explore some remote areas of Grand Canyon himself, and he agreed to be on standby if we needed him for our mission. He took our vehicle since we wouldn't need it.

Inside the train depot, hundreds of people bustled about buying train tickets and souvenirs. We were guided to outdoor bleachers overlooking a set done up like a small western town, and were entertained with a wild west show! Cowboys on horseback rode onto the set, dressed just like they would have been in the 1800s. They wore long trench coats, cowboy hats, and boot spurs, and they had holsters with pistols in them on their hips. Without having to time travel, they showed us a pretty good depiction of what life was like as a western cowboy. They had a shootout, and of course, the good guys won. Then it was finally time to board the train.

"All aboard!" the conductor shouted.

We walked past an old locomotive as we hurried to board, and a sign explained that it was a Shay No. 5 built in 1923. It used coal and wood to operate its engine.

"In 1901 this train line was completed and quickly became the best way to get to and from Grand Canyon. Prior to the train line, you would have had to ride in a stagecoach, which took longer and would cost more money," T2 explained.

"I have tickets to ride in coach. There are first class seats and dome view seats, too, but I thought it would be best if we stuck together," Sydney explained.

We kept walking along the tracks and we passed by several cars before we came upon our coach car. There was a conductor standing near it, and he was dressed like it was the 1900s. He wore a blue hat, a blue suit, a white shirt, and a red tie. He took our tickets with a smile as we boarded the train. The entire train was original, and our car was vintage 1950s. It looked like each car on the train varied in age.

"By 1968, most people drove to Grand Canyon National Park and the train stopped service due to a lack of passengers. But a new company started the train service back up again in 1989 and according to their website, the train helps prevent 50,000 cars from entering the park each year while also providing a fun, historical way to arrive in Grand Canyon National Park," T2 said, gesturing toward the historically accurate seats and windows.

"What's wrong with driving into the park?" Hug-a-Bug asked.

"With over five million visitors to Grand Canyon each year, there are not enough parking spots for everyone," T2 replied. "In addition to this train line, Grand Canyon offers a free shuttle bus. So, visitors don't really need their cars. They can ride the shuttle bus, or they can walk, hike, bike, or even ride mules!"

"Some pretty famous people took this train to Grand Canyon," Papa Lewis added.

"Really? Who?" I inquired, wondering if maybe they'd sat right where I was sitting!

"Well, you had your fair share of presidents: Theodore Roosevelt (also known as Teddy), William Howard Taft, Franklin Delano Roosevelt (FDR), and Dwight Eisenhower. The most famous naturalist, John Muir, rode this train. So did many modern celebrities and well-known business tycoons!"

"That's pretty cool!"

"Theodore Roosevelt is recognized for playing a significant role in establishing Grand Canyon as a national park," Papa Lewis added.

Our train car jerked forward, and a loud whistle burst signaled that we were on our way toward Grand Canyon National Park. We picked up speed and in no time at all we were chugging along at a fast clip.

The hostess in our car was dressed to match the car's vintage 1950s style. She shared a wealth of knowledge about the terrain as it surged by outside our windows, and told us to keep an eye out for wildlife, including mountain lions (Hug-a-Bug's eyes got real big when she heard that!). For once, we didn't need to use our time travel skills to experience the past. There even was a genuine early-1900s wild west sheriff on board to keep our train safe from outlaws! The landscape shifted as we passed into a ponderosa pine forest; I pointed out every mule deer and elk I could spot as they grazed in the pines' tranquil shade.

The hostess explained that we were approaching the Grand Canyon Depot inside Grand Canyon National Park. T2 whispered something to Papa Lewis, who then stood up and waved at Hug-a-Bug and me, gesturing for us to follow him. We walked together through several train cars until we found one without passengers. Papa Lewis sat us down, and I knew it was time for us to finalize our game plan.

"When we reach the station, T2 and Sydney will stay out of sight. We don't want Blaze and Song to know that they're here with you. You'll meet up with the school group at the Bright Angel Lodge, which is just a short walk from the train depot. The rest of us plan to stay in the El Tovar Hotel nearby." Papa Lewis looked at each of us in turn.

"Got it," I said, and Hug-a-Bug nodded. "We'll know where to find you if we need help."

The train jerked to a stop in front of a rustic railroad depot, which was built out of logs and painted a traditional dark brown national park color. Another wood and rock masonry building, that resembled a Swiss alpine hotel, was perched above the tree canopy just behind the depot. "Is that the lodge?" I asked Papa Lewis as I motioned toward it.

"Yep, that's the El Tovar Hotel. It's a historic lodge that was built along the edge of the South Rim," he responded.

Hundreds of passengers snaked off the train and ascended a set of stairs in the direction of the El Tovar Hotel. Our parents, T2, Sydney, and Grandma all mixed into the crowd. Papa Lewis, Hug-a-Bug, and I followed after them, trying to blend in with the surge of tourists. The El Tovar Hotel came into view over to our left. So many people were wandering around! I noticed an ancient-looking two-story sandstone building not too far from the lodge, also along the South Rim. "What's that building there?"

"That's the Hopi House, and over there is Verkamp's Visitor Center," Papa Lewis explained, pointing out another structure to me that was right next to the Hopi House. It suddenly sank in: I was standing just feet from the rim of Grand Canyon; how amazing! I wanted to stay there, looking out over the rim, watching the sun move in the sky, but there was so much more to do and see.

"We'll be sure to explore everything that your school adventure group doesn't get to," Papa Lewis said as if he knew exactly what was going through my head in that moment.

"What did Teddy Roosevelt do to help make this a national park?" I asked him.

"Well, say, we've got a few minutes, don't we? Let's go back in time and find out!" Papa Lewis grinned, and I grinned back, excited to use my powers. "May 6th, 1903, to be exact."

The three of us ducked out of sight and found a quiet, secluded area in the shadow of El Tovar Hotel. I placed my hand on our family journal and said, "Take us back to May 6th, 1903!"

Everything went dark, a gust of wind knocked us

back, and then it was light again. We were now all dressed in formal clothing like what we had worn when we rafted with Major John Wesley Powell. The buildings we'd seen before we jumped back in time were almost all gone. It looked like the El Tovar Hotel was under construction. Just like in our time, there were people standing along the South Rim of Grand Canyon to stare out at its raw beauty. We walked over and joined them. The view was just as stunning in 1903 as it was in our present. The canyon was so big, it made me feel smaller than small.

I squinted, noticing something in the distance, no, some*one*: a stout man with glasses and a mustache. He wore a wide-brimmed hat, a suit jacket, and a scarf tied around his neck, and his pants were tucked into knee-high boots. He looked like he was ready to mount a horse and blaze a trail across the desert, just like that! Based on the small group of alert men in plainclothes that stood near him with pistols in holsters, and the way murmuring visitors glanced at him as they passed by, it looked like he was somebody important.

"That's Teddy," Papa Lewis whispered to me, confirming it.

We joined the crowd that had gathered near the president to hear what he was going to say. Teddy pulled out a piece of paper and stepped up to the podium. The crowd immediately quieted. As the president began to give his speech, I noticed a young boy and girl standing nearby. They didn't seem to have parents with them, and they seemed confused. They looked familiar to me somehow, but I definitely hadn't seen them before.

"Sydney," Hug-a-Bug said softly; she'd noticed them, too. "I think they kinda look like Sydney. Do you think they're Blaze and Song?"

We all walked together towards them to getter a closer look, but as we approached, they walked swiftly away and around a bend. By the time we turned the corner, they were gone. We returned to the group gathered silently around the president and caught the very last part of the president's speech.

"Let this great wonder of nature remain as it now is!" Teddy crowed. "Do nothing to mar its grandeur, sublimity, and loveliness. You cannot improve on it. But what you can do is keep it for your children, your children's children, and all who come after you, as the one great sight which every American should see."

Everyone standing around the president clapped and cheered. Papa Lewis, Hug-a-Bug, and I slipped away and walked into a stand of trees out of sight. I placed my hand on the journal in my pocket as we all huddled close and I said, "Take us back to the present."

Again, the world went dark and a gust of wind blew. A bright light made me squint, and I lifted my hand to shade my eyes. We were all crouched next to the El Tovar Hotel wearing our modern clothes once again.

"Wow, we witnessed national park history!" Hug-a-Bug gasped.

"The president gave that speech to try and protect Grand Canyon from development. It may have stopped some developers, but it was impossible to stop Grand Canyon from becoming a tourist attraction. Hotels, restaurants, mines, and anything people could make money from continued to sprout up all across the canyon. So, in 1908, Teddy used his presidential powers to declare Grand Canyon a national monument, because the National Park Service had not been created yet. Teddy's own actions led to the creation of Grand Canyon National Park," Papa Lewis explained.

"Do you think those two kids we saw were Blaze and Song?" I asked Papa Lewis and Hug-a-Bug.

"They were too far away to get a really good look," Hug-a-Bug answered. "I'm not sure, honestly."

"I'm not sure either," Papa Lewis sighed. "But regard-less, you two better head over and meet up with your school group. We're staying right next door to you guys in the El Tovar Hotel. It has a Teddy Roosevelt room in the restaurant. That room will be our meet up point if you need us for anything."

We hugged Papa Lewis goodbye (for now). Hug-a-Bug and I grabbed our backpacks and followed the signs to the Bright Angel Lodge. Our mission was offi-cially in full swing!

CHAPTER 5

GRAND CANYON ADVENTURE CAMP

As we approached the porch steps of the Bright Angel Lodge, I noticed two adults standing near the entrance with matching t-shirts that said "Adventure Club Staff." Lanyards hung around their necks with their staff IDs dangling at the ends.

"Hi there!" one of them yelled, waving at us and motioning for us both to come closer. "I'm Tony and this is Harper. You must be Tommy and Jenny, or wait, you prefer Bubba Jones and Hug-a-Bug, right?"

"Yep, Bubba Jones and Hug-a-Bug. Those are our adventure names," I answered.

"Welcome to our Adventure Club, and welcome to Grand Canyon," Harper greeted.

"Thank you! We're excited to join you guys," Hug-a-Bug replied.

"Yeah, this is a pretty special place. Let's get you both settled into your rooms. Right now, all the other adventurers are gathered behind the lodge getting their gear ready for today's activities. Our first adventure is a geological walk through time. We have a lot more activities planned as well. How does that sound?" Tony asked us.

"We love traveling through time," I said, grinning at Hug-a-Bug. She giggled. If they only knew how much I sincerely meant that we love to time travel.

"You guys joined us at a perfect time. Yesterday, we rode the train into the park and checked into this wonderful historic lodge. The next few days will be filled with lots of adventure. All the other kids are paired up in lodge rooms, and you've been assigned some, too, let's see." Harper pulled out a roster and flipped through it, scanning the pages for our names. "Bubba Jones, you'll stay with Blaze and Hug-a-Bug, you'll stay with Song. They are brother and sister just like you two, so we hope that this will be a good match!"

We couldn't have had better luck. "Awesome! Thank you," I said, excited to meet these kids we'd heard so much about.

Tony and Harper led us to our lodge rooms to drop off our gear and then they led us to the terrace behind the Bright Angel Lodge where the school adventure group had gathered. There were only eight or so students other than Hug-a-Bug and me, so it was pretty easy to see Blaze and Song. They didn't seem to recognize us, and they looked just as curious about us as all the other students did. Tony wasted no time introducing us to the group.

"Everyone, this is Bubba Jones and Hug-a-Bug. They're visiting students and they're going to join us on our adventures. Do your best to make them feel welcome, okay? Now that we're all here, we should jump right in!" Tony said.

"Our very own Branson spearheaded a Grand Canyon geology project for his independent study," Harper continued, following Tony's lead. "He partnered with a student by the name of Arthur from Bar Harbor, Maine, which is clear across the U.S. in Acadia National Park. They taught each other about the geology of the parks they live near. Branson's going to share his findings with us, and they involve some time travel! How cool is that? Give it up for Branson!"

We all clapped, and just as I was about to turn to Hug-a-Bug she nudged me with her shoulder. She looked about as nervous as I felt.

If you've followed us on our other adventures, you know that Hug-a-Bug and I were just in Acadia National Park helping our cousin Arthur (who also has our family's powers) and his sister solve a mystery, and now here we are in Grand Canyon, about to listen to Branson talk about a project he worked on with Arthur involving *time travel*. Things were getting interesting. There was a chance that the Arthur from Maine that Branson worked with wasn't our cousin. But how many Arthurs are there that are our age, from Bar Harbor, and doing "time travel" projects?

"Arthur wouldn't tell his secret, would he?" Hug-a-Bug whispered to me.

"I don't think so," I replied under my breath. "Let's wait and see what Branson says."

Branson stood up to speak to us. He seemed a little nervous standing in front of his fellow students, but once he started talking, he became more and more relaxed. "I thought a project about old rocks would be boring," he began, and that made us laugh a little. "That was, until I partnered with Arthur from across the country. The aim of my project was to partner with another student from near another national park that had never been to Grand Canyon and have us teach each other about the geology of the parks we live near. What happened next was amazing! He taught me about the geology of his park using *time travel!*"

I held my breath.

Branson chuckled a little and lifted his hands. "Okay, okay, we didn't *really* time travel," he clarified, and Hug-a-Bug and I both immediately sighed with relief, "but the way Arthur described the creation and the formation of the rocks and terrain somehow made me *feel like* I traveled through time. It was as if I was right there, watching it all with him. He was a great teacher."

Hug-a-Bug and I looked at each other and at the same time we both quietly uttered, "Cousin Arthur." *We need to let Papa Lewis know about this,* I thought.

"Before we 'time travel' like I did with Arthur, we should review some Grand Canyon geology facts that I learned from the park geology museum," Branson continued. "Geologists classify rocks into three main types: igneous, sedimentary, and metamorphic. Igneous rocks form from molten rock, either lava or magma, when it cools and solidifies either above or below the ground. Sedimentary rocks are made from lots of pieces, such as sand grains, weathered from older rocks that are then deposited in layers and stick together over time. The third type of rock, metamorphic, involves the change of sedimentary, igneous, or even already existing metamorphic rock into something new!"

"What makes the rocks change?" Hug-a-Bug asked.

Branson seemed excited to respond; he definitely came prepared for his presentation. "Metamorphic rocks are rocks that have 'morphed' into different rocks because they experienced increases in heat, pressure, or both. For instance, when a blob of magma rises upward into cooler rocks, it bakes them, which changes the types and sizes of their crystals. These changes can also happen as a result of squeezing rocks that are caught between colliding tectonic plates. More heat and more pressure cause bigger changes to the original rock. This process is called metamorphism."

"Wow, Branson sure does know his stuff," Hug-a-Bug said to me softly. "He talks like a university professor or something."

"Earth was created approximately 4.6 billion years ago. The oldest rocks here in Grand Canyon are 1.8 billion years old. Guess where the oldest rocks are?" Branson asked. Hug-a-Bug raised her hand and he pointed to her.

"At the bottom of Grand Canyon?" she answered, some hesitation in her voice.

"That's right! The oldest layer is at the bottom and the newest layer is at the top, just like a layered cake," Branson said as he pulled a cover off a layered cake sitting on a mini portable table next to him. He cut a slice of cake and turned the platter around, revealing the inner layers to us. It was one funky-looking cake! The bottom cake layer was chocolate, the middle layer was vanilla, and the top layer was strawberry. The icings between the cake layers were different colors, too.

"The baker placed this first cake layer at the bottom. That's the oldest layer. Then they added a layer of icing and then they placed another cake layer on. Then they added *more* icing, then another cake layer, and then *more* icing, you get it," Branson explained as he pointed at each layer. He finished cutting up the cake into slices and Tony and Harper helped get the slices onto plates and gave one to each of us. Science is always more fun with food! But we were told not to eat the cake just yet, so all of us waited for Branson to finish his presentation.

"Look out at Grand Canyon. Do you see the different layers of rock? See how they vary in color and thickness? Each layer tells a story, and the science of studying these layers is called stratigraphy. Scientists who specialize in stratigraphy describe the rock layers of a given area and how their layers are arranged by drawing detailed vertical stacks that they call stratigraphic columns. The layers are filled with fossils which help scientist figure out the age of each layer." Branson stopped, looking at all of us, before he realized he'd forgotten to say something important. "Oh yeah, you can eat your cake now!"

I scooped a piece of cake into my mouth and was surprised when I bit into something chewy and gummy. It tasted like a Snickers bar! I took another bite and there was a chunk in it with a different texture. It had a chocolatey taste and was kinda chewy: a Tootsie Roll!

"Did anyone discover Snickers and Tootsie Roll fossils yet?" Branson asked.

Everyone raised their hands.

"Um yeah, and they were tasty," Hug-a-Bug answered, which made us all laugh.

"A geologist helped me come up with the cake idea to explain stratigraphy," Branson explained, happy with how well he was doing so far. "We're almost ready to head out on our time travel adventure now that you have some background about the rocks."

"That was a great presentation, and the cake was amazing. But Branson, do scientists know how Grand Canyon was created?" I asked.

Branson nodded. "About 60 million years ago, this entire area was lifted up by plate tectonics. Usually when that happens, rocks crumble and break apart. At least, that's what happened in the Rocky Mountains east of here. But somehow this entire area remained flat and intact. It's known as the Colorado Plateau. This was a key event that led to the formation of Grand Canyon. If you look across the canyon, you'll notice that it's very flat and even all along the rim." Branson paused and looked over at Tony and Harper. "But um, if you want to find out the rest of your answer, you'll have to walk through time the way Arthur told me to find out when Grand Canyon was formed. Is everyone ready?"

Tony took it from there. "Okay everyone, this adventure is an easy stroll along the rim trail, it'll be about 1.7 miles. The Trail of Time begins up ahead at Verkamp's Visitor Center and ends at the Yavapai Geology Museum."

"We're standing on the rim trail right now," Harper explained, motioning to the path near us. "It's paved the entire length and it's flat, so it'll be more of a stroll than a hike. Nonetheless, we all need to stay hydrated and protected from the sun. So, everyone please apply a lot of sunscreen, put on your brimmed hats, and take along your water bottles. We'll shuttle back to our lodge on the park bus."

We followed the rim trail along the edge of Grand Canyon and wound behind the El Tovar Hotel. Then we came up on the Hopi House; I remembered it from when we arrived. From up close, it looked even more as if it just sprouted up out of the rock of the canyon itself since it was made out of rich red sandstone. It was several stories tall with wooden ladders set up on the exterior for climbing up to each floor, and it had a bunch of little square window holes. Tony noticed that Hug-a-Bug and I had stopped to gaze at the structure and joined us.

"That's the Hopi House," he told us. "Most everyone in the Adventure Club has been inside it since they live here. You should check it out with your family while you're here if you can. It was designed by Mary Colter, an architect commissioned by Fred Harvey to create a souvenir shop where people could buy art created by indigenous artisans. Ms. Colter designed it to look as much like a Hopi pueblo as possible."

As Tony gave us more details about the Hopi House, I felt like someone was staring at me. I glanced over my shoulder and I could see Papa Lewis, Grandma Lewis, Dad, and Mom sitting in rocking chairs on the lodge's porch.

"I need to use the restroom, excuse me," I lied as I ran off towards the El Tovar Hotel. As soon as my feet hit the steps, I looked up and caught Papa Lewis's eyes. He nodded and motioned inside; we'd meet in the designated place.

The hotel was made from wood and rock, and the lobby felt like the inside of a hunting lodge. The interior log walls were stained a dark brown. A large stone fireplace filled one corner of the room, and above me was a tall vaulted wood ceiling with log rafters and dimly lit chandeliers. Mounted heads of moose, elk, and deer hung on the walls. Guests lounged in chairs and couches scattered throughout the lobby. I stepped up to the front desk and asked where the Roosevelt Room was. I followed the concierge's directions to a small private dining room attached to the hotel restaurant. Papa Lewis entered moments later.

"We need to talk," I began as he came over and sat down. "Arthur from Acadia has communicated with one of the students in our adventure group. I don't know what to make of it, but I thought I should let you know."

"Hm. Arthur. I don't know what to make of that either, but we'll summon you and Hug-a-Bug both for a meet up later today and we can talk more then. You should get back to your adventure for now," Papa Lewis said.

I nodded and hurriedly walked out of the hotel, down the steps, and back to the group of students waiting by the Hopi House. As soon as I reached the group, Branson began leading us further along the rim trail until we stopped in front of Verkamp's Visitor Center.

"Bubba Jones and Hug-a-Bug, you'll want to check out Verkamp's Visitor Center sometime while you're here, but right now, Branson's about to take us back in time," Tony said, winking at us. "Okay, Branson, take it away!"

Branson took a deep breath, then continued his presentation. "For the next 1.7 miles, think of every big step you take as the equivalent of a million years. Imagine that we're starting the trail of time 2,000 million years ago, okay? We're going to walk forward in time until we reach the present day."

Hug-a-Bug and I looked at each other and shrugged. It seemed pretty neat; another fun way to "travel through time" without ever leaving the present! We tried to imagine ourselves 2,000 million years ago, just like Branson said.

Branson led us a few steps further along the rim trail to a grey rock mounted on a cement platform. Etched in the platform was an inscription: "Elves Chasm Gneiss 1,840 million years old."

"This is the oldest rock in Grand Canyon. Rocks like this one can be found at the bottom, or the 'basement,' of Grand Canyon," Branson explained.

Hug-a-Bug and I watched Blaze and Song closely. If they were curious about any time periods we walked past, we thought that they might try to time travel with the magical lens, which they must have if they were the kids we saw when we went back to see Teddy Roosevelt. But so far, it didn't seem like they had the lens at all. They were both chatting and having fun with the other kids in the group, showing no sign of splitting away from everyone else.

We continued and stopped at another rock mounted on a platform with another etched description: "Rama Schist 1,755 million years old." A few more steps and we passed another: "Zoroaster Granite 1,740 million years old." Then another: "Vishnu Schist 1,745 million years old." And *another*: "Brahma Schist 1,750 million years old." These rock mounts were displayed all along the entire trail. By the time we approached the end of the walk, it really began to sink in how long it took for all of these rocks to form, and how much sheer time had to pass for us to see the canyon as it is today. We started our walk 2,000 million years in the past. By the time we were near the end of our 1.7-mile walk we *still* hadn't reached the point in time when Grand Canyon was created! We encountered 270-million-year-old fossilized sea life forms at the Kaibab Limestone rock. The dinosaurs hadn't even walked the earth yet; dinosaurs wouldn't occur until even further into the future, around 245 million years ago! The Mesozoic layers, when the dinosaurs walked the earth, do not exist in Grand Canyon. The group stopped again as Branson explained all of this. Hug-a-Bug nudged me and motioned away from the others, so I followed her away from the group to talk.

"Bubba Jones, are you thinking what I'm thinking? Those sea fossils mean that there was an ancient ocean here. We should time travel back to the ancient ocean and take a swim," Hug-a-Bug whispered, wide-eyed.

"The group will notice we're gone and we won't be able to keep an eye on Blaze and Song," I countered, glancing over my shoulder at the others. "We should focus on our mission."

"Oh, it'll only be for a few minutes. Come on Bubba, don't you want to take a swim and see what this place was like before Grand Canyon was formed?" Hug-a-Bug pleaded. "It'll be so amazing to see all these cool creatures alive and free instead of fossilized."

She knew I loved swimming, and it really did sound too good to resist. *It'll only be for a few minutes,* I thought, glancing once more at the group before nodding to Hug-a-Bug. "Okay, let's walk out of view around that bend in the trail, quickly."

We found a spot in a stand of trees hidden from the students and counselors. Hug-a-Bug and I huddled together, and I said, "Take us back to 270 million years in the past."

Everything went dark, a gust of wind pushed against me, and then it was light again. I nervously peered around, blinking to help my eyes adjust.

Grand Canyon was *gone*!

Hug-a-Bug and I stood along a vast seashore and looked out at a body of water that stretched as far as the eye could see. The sea was alive with all the fossilized creatures we'd just seen in rock before, but even with them darting and splashing in the waters, we felt completely and utterly alone. It was warm but not quite as hot as it was back in the present. Hug-a-Bug and I waded into the water up to our knees, ready to take a quick swim with some ancient creatures, but I suddenly got the feeling we weren't the only humans out here after all. *What's that?* I thought.

A flash had lit up the sky above us and there was a strong gust of wind. All of a sudden, I heard distant voices. It was hard to identify whose voices though. One thing was for sure: they were definitely time travelers.

CHAPTER 6

STEPPING THROUGH TIME

"Hug-a-Bug, get underwater so they don't see us!"
I said. She nodded and we immediately took
deep breaths and submerged ourselves beneath
the waves.

We held hands to stay together as the current pulled
us. I really wanted to find out who the time travelers were,
but getting closer would risk blowing our cover before
gathering all the facts and understanding the whole situation. When we'd held our breath for as long as we could,
I shot up to the surface, pulling Hug-a-Bug up with me.
We gasped for air and looked up and down the beach

for any sign of the time travelers. The sun had come out from behind a cloud, and it was so bright against the water that it was hard to see anything, but from across the water we heard someone say something.

"Could this time travel magic stop the formation of Grand Canyon?"

Then there was another flash of bright light and we were shoved underwater by an invisible force that vanished as quickly as it had come. They had gone back to their present.

Hug-a-Bug couldn't contain herself, her eyes wide with fear. "What just happened? Did you hear what that person said? They're going to stop the formation of Grand Canyon! Do you think they saw us?"

I placed a hand on her shoulder. "One thing at a time. Let's get back to the present and see if we can figure out who that was." We huddled together and I said, "Take us back to the present."

Everything went dark, the invisible force pushed against us, and then it was light again. Hug-a-Bug and I were back in the present, hidden by the same stand of trees we'd left from before. We walked up the trail and easily caught up to the rest of the Adventure Club, as we'd returned to the exact same moment in time we'd left from.

"Did you guys go to the restroom?" Tony asked us as we joined the group.

"No, we wanted to do a little more research back in time," I answered.

Tony sighed. "I know this is an interesting and

exciting place, but we need to stay together, okay? Don't wander off."

"Sorry, we won't do it again."

Hug-a-Bug and I scanned the group for signs of someone that just transported themselves 270 million years into the past and back. Whenever we time travel from the past to the present, our clothing changes right back to what it was before we'd left so we're easily able to blend back in. The only definite visual sign that someone may have time traveled would be in their behavior, if they were acting nervous or mysterious or strange. Song and Blaze were with the rest of the adventure group and they didn't appear to be suspicious at all. I carefully looked over each person in our adventure group for anything that looked unusual or resembled the missing time travel lens. Everyone had water bottles. Some of the kids had cell phones and some of them had binoculars. Nothing out of the ordinary. At least, not yet!

We were approaching Yavapai Point and the Yavapai Geology Museum, a sign that the Trail of Time was about to end. We all stopped and stood around Branson to learn about the final bit of Grand Canyon's geological history.

"Dinosaurs walked the earth about 245 million years ago and became extinct around 66 million years ago. Although, it should be noted that the Mesozoic layers, when the dinosaurs walked the earth, do not exist in Grand Canyon," Branson began. Everyone in the group was present, which meant that even if Song and Blaze *did* have the time travel lens, they had no interest in going back to experience the dinosaurs, thank goodness. That's one period of time I did *not* want to mess with, both dangerous and scary. Branson took a few more steps along the path and stopped again.

"The Colorado Plateau began its uplift right about here, 60 million years ago," he explained before walking on. All of us followed. He then stopped just steps before the completion of the Trail of Time. "These are the last few steps of the entire 1.7-mile Trail of Time, and these last few steps represent five or six million years ago when the Colorado River began to carve Grand Canyon. Spring runoff and flooding did a lot to shape the canyon with the help of tributaries. Five or six million years is a relatively short amount of time compared to the 1.84 billion years, the age of the first rock we saw on this trail. Grand Canyon is still being carved today. Next we're going to check out the Yavapai Geology Museum. This museum is loaded with even more facts about Grand Canyon, and it's where I did most of my research for this presentation. Thank you all for coming along on my time travel adventure!" Branson concluded.

We all clapped, and several students complimented Branson for his professorial presentation, and then we walked into the Yavapai Geology Museum to cap off our geology adventure. The museum was another stone building made to blend into the surrounding Grand Canyon landscape. Windows provided a panoramic view of the canyon and plaques described the geology of some of the rock you could see outside. The place was riddled with interactive exhibits that gave even more details about the creation of this geologic marvel. Hug-a-Bug and I had so much fun exploring the museum that it wasn't until Tony and Harper announced that it was time to board the shuttle bus that I looked around and realized that Blaze, Song, and Branson weren't with us.

I tapped Hug-a-Bug on the shoulder. She looked over at me and immediately noticed what I'd noticed. We began searching for Branson, Blaze, and Song all over the museum. When we didn't find them inside, we walked outside and retraced our steps toward the Trail of Time. Branson, Blaze, and Song came around a bend in the trail just as we were getting close to it.

"Hey, guys!" I greeted, waving at them. "What are you all doing out here? The adventure group'll be boarding the shuttle bus any minute now."

"I took Blaze and Song back along the Trail of Time 'cause they wanted to talk more about a specific point in Grand Canyon's history," Branson explained.

"What point?" Hug-a-Bug asked.

"The point of its creation," Song answered. She really did look a lot like Sydney, but with shorter hair and lighter eyes.

"Why? What did you guys talk about?" Hug-a-Bug asked, hoping to discover a clue to solve our mission.

Branson leaned toward us. "Grand Canyon is such an amazing natural wonder," he began, his eyes glinting. "Imagine if we could *really* go back in time and witness the Colorado River cutting its way through the rock, creating the canyon. What would happen if something stopped Grand Canyon from forming? What would this place look like today?"

Did Branson, Blaze, and Song time travel into the past *together*? Were all three of them up to something? What could I say to get one of them to slip up and reveal what they know, or to convince them to let Hug-a-Bug and me in on their secret?

"That would be so cool if you could actually go back in time, but you can't," I answered, shrugging. "Even if you could, you wouldn't be able to notice the changes day-to-day of something that took five or six *million* years to create! It would be like watching a slow-motion video of paint drying. If Grand Canyon never formed, I imagine this whole place would just look like a flat dry desert. And what could possibly stop it from forming?"

Blaze looked past me toward the museum. Even though he and Song were twins, his face was very different from hers, though the family resemblance was still obvious. He had dark eyes, and while Song seemed calm, he seemed fidgety. "Come on, Song, let's get on the shuttle bus." He started walking and Song followed him, glancing once over her shoulder at us.

"He's right, we better catch the shuttle," Branson said, following Blaze and Song back to the museum.

"We'll be right there!" I called after Branson. Hug-a-Bug and I waited until they were all out of hearing range before we started brainstorming.

"I think they're actually trying to stop Grand Canyon

from forming for some reason. What do you think?" Hug-a-Bug asked.

"I'm not sure. We need to share all this with T2, Sydney, and Papa Lewis right away," I responded.

We both trotted to catch up with Branson, Blaze, and Song. Harper and Tony were standing on the sidewalk by the shuttle bus door, waiting for us.

"Bubba Jones, Hug-a-Bug, this is for you," Tony said as he handed me an envelope. "Also, your parents let me know that they're going to take you and Hug-a-Bug out for some sightseeing later this afternoon. I hope they take you to the Hopi House and Verkamp's Visitor Center."

"We're going to ask them to take us there for sure!" Hug-a-Bug insisted as we boarded the bus. It was filled with tourists, some of them couples, some of them families, some of them on their own. We found two open seats near the rest of our group and the bus departed. A few minutes later, it screeched to a halt at the main visitor center, and we all hopped off the orange line bus and boarded a waiting blue line bus which whisked us to a stop near the Bright Angel Lodge. Once we all got off the bus, we gathered around Harper and Tony.

"We have sack lunches for everyone inside," Harper told us "After lunch, you can all have an hour of individual time before we regroup for our afternoon program."

"What's planned for the afternoon program?" I asked. "Is it okay that we're missing it?"

Tony waved his hand. "Don't worry! We're going to prepare our gear and review plans for our overnight backpack trip down into Grand Canyon. Your parents informed us that you and Hug-a-Bug have backpacked before, so we'll just catch you up on what we discuss after the program, before we all head to bed. So far, we have one parent joining us as a chaperone. I know it's last-minute, but if your parents have an interest in the trip they're welcome to join us as chaperones, too, especially since they have hiking experience."

"That sounds great; I'll let them know. Our grandpa and grandma are here as well and they might be interested, too. Thank you!" I replied.

While everyone was busy grabbing their lunch, Hug-a-Bug and I slipped up to the lodge room that I'd be sharing with Blaze. Hug-a-Bug stood watch at the door while I tore open the seal of the envelope and unfolded a paper with a coded message inside, a Caesar Code like all the other messages. We have other ways of communicating secretly, too, if our code was ever compromised.

QEFP FP   MI   XOQERO   AFA   ZLOOBPMLKA
        TFQE   YOXKPLK

JBBQ   VLR   FK   QEB   ILYYV   XQ   QTL MJ

I pulled out my decoder and went to work deciphering the message.

Plain: THIS IS   PL   ARTHUR   DID
          CORRESPOND   WITH   BRANSON

Cipher: QEFP   FP   MI   XOQERO   AFA
           ZLOOBPMLKA   TFQE YOXKPLK

Plain: MEET YOU IN THE LOBBY AT TWO PM
Cipher: JBBQ VLR FK QEB ILYYV XQ QTL MJ

Plain	A	B	C	D	E	F	G	H	I	J	K	L	M
Cipher	X	Y	Z	A	B	C	D	E	F	G	H	I	J

Plain	N	O	P	Q	R	S	T	U	V	W	X	Y	Z
Cipher	K	L	M	N	O	P	Q	R	S	T	U	V	W

"What's it say, Bubba Jones?" Hug-a-Bug whispered.

"It's a message from Papa Lewis. Our cousin Arthur did correspond with Branson. Papa Lewis said he will meet us in the Bright Angel lobby at 2:00 PM," I whispered back.

"Bubba, do you think our cousin and Branson are involved with the missing time travel lens?"

"Let's wait to talk about that until we see Papa Lewis later. We should see what he knows before we come to any conclusions."

It doesn't make sense that our cousin Arthur would want to steal time travel magic from someone; he has his own time travel ability! We still had very little information about the missing time travel lens, and it seemed like the more we learned, the less we knew.

CHAPTER 7

DESIGNED TO BLEND IN

We slipped back down to the terrace behind the lodge to have lunch with the adventure group. No one seemed to notice that we were even gone. We grabbed our lunch sacks and found ourselves a stone seat where we could eat and look out over the canyon, a perfect view. Once we were settled, Blaze and Song came over with their lunches.

"Can we sit with you guys?" Blaze asked.

"Of course!" Hug-a-Bug said, and Song giggled. "Tony and Harper told us that we're rooming with each other. That means we have to be friends!"

We made room for them on the bench, and they asked us about our hiking experience and what gear we brought along. I explained that Hug-a-Bug and I were going to miss the afternoon program for some sightseeing with family.

"If we go over anything you don't already know in the afternoon program, we'll fill you in," Blaze offered.

"Yeah, it's good that you'll be able to do stuff with your family while you're all here together," Song chimed in.

Blaze and Song were really nice. I wished I could simply ask them if they knew anything about the time travel lens, and just tell them straight out that we're actually relatives.

As we chatted and laughed and ate our lunches, a park volunteer, dressed in khaki pants, a dark green shirt, and a khaki hat, stopped along the rock wall near the rim of Grand Canyon. He held a large metal antenna, like what people used to perch on their roofs to get a TV signal before cable and satellite TV. Tourists began to gather near him to get a closer look at what he was doing. They pointed up at the sky and snapped pictures. A large black-winged object flew high in the air over the canyon. Was the park volunteer flying a drone?

I stood up and walked closer to where the volunteer stood. He was being peppered with questions from the tourists who'd approached him. "I'm monitoring that California condor up there," he said to one of them as he pointed up towards the sky. "This antenna helps us track the radio tag fixed to its wing, and each tagged bird has a different identification number."

I heard Blaze, Song, and Hug-a-Bug come up beside me. "Here," Blaze said, passing me his binoculars so I could get a closer look. With the binoculars, I could see that the winged thing was definitely a bird, and its head was a bright orange color!

The park volunteer continued to answer tourists' questions. "The California condor's wingspan can be as wide as nine and a half feet. In 1982, they were nearly extinct with just 22 birds in the wild. A massive conservation program was put into place and the 22 remaining birds were taken into captivity. They only lay one egg every one or two years and they don't start laying eggs until they're older than six. They're scavengers and eat any dead meat they can find, which means mostly bighorn sheep and mule deer. Their population was almost wiped out thanks to lead bullets that hunters left in their uncollected kills, which the condors would eat for food. The conservation program was a success, however, and now California condors are back in the wild, over 300 of them! They nest on ledges and in caves, and they seldom stay in the same place twice."

The condor glided and arced over the canyon before flying off. Once it had gone too far away, the tourists began to disperse.

"That's the coolest bird I've ever seen," I said to Song, and she nodded in agreement.

"I hope it continues to thrive in the wild," she added.

"Me, too," the park volunteer chimed in as he packed up his antenna and walked off, maybe to track another condor.

We saw Tony approaching us and walked up to meet him; he reminded Hug-a-Bug and me to be in the lobby at two o'clock to meet up with our parents. There was still some time left before we had to go, so we sat and continued talking with Blaze and Song, enjoying Grand Canyon's views all the while.

At two o' clock, Hug-a-Bug and I stepped into the Bright Angel Lodge and walked to the main lobby. The interior was built out of logs and stained a dark brown. It had a stone floor and bright indigenous artwork on the wall. Tourists stood in line at the front desk. Across from the main doors stood a massive stone fireplace with a bird painting above the mantel. An antique stagecoach was on display along the side wall across from the front desk. A small group of hikers toting full-fledged backpacks loaded with all the provisions for an overnight adventure stood at a small counter tucked in the corner to the left of the main door. A sign above the counter read "Bus Tours, Mule Rides, Phantom Ranch Reservations."

"Y'all are in luck; we had a cancellation and there are four bunks available at Phantom Ranch tonight," a clerk told the hikers from behind the counter as she stared at her computer screen.

"Awesome! Thank you!" one of the hikers said. As their group headed out and pushed the front door open, in walked Papa Lewis, Grandma, Mom, and Dad. We all hugged and chatted for a minute.

"Before we go anywhere, we need to check this out," Papa Lewis insisted. He led us through the lobby and into the history room off on the left. He pointed to a portrait of Mary Elizabeth Jane Colter on the wall with a description of who she was below it.

"Mary Colter designed this building and several other structures here in Grand Canyon. She was the chief architect and designer for the Fred Harvey Company. It was rare for a woman to have a prestigious career in the early 1900s and she did her job so well, her style influenced modern-day architects. She designed with Grand Canyon's history and beauty in mind," Papa Lewis explained.

"Why was it rare for women to have prestigious jobs?" Hug-a-Bug asked.

"It used to be that most men went out to work and most women stayed home and solely did housework," Papa Lewis answered, and Hug-a-Bug made a face. "But that didn't stop Mary Colter from pursuing her architectural career. Fred Harvey was a growing company and she received a job offer from them. They were building railroads, hotels, and restaurants along the train routes. The rest is history."

"It's good things have changed for the better. I want to meet Mary Colter!" Hug-a-Bug exclaimed.

"I figured you would," Papa Lewis said with a grin. "Bubba Jones, take us back to 1935."

We all walked outside and found a place out of view, and once we were all gathered into a circle, I said, "Take us back to 1935."

Everything went dark. A gust of wind blew. Then, it was daylight again. I opened my eyes and looked around. Our clothing had changed to 1930s era dress. I wore long pants, a long-sleeve shirt, and a wide brim hat; so did Dad and Papa Lewis. All the women wore ankle-length dresses, leather shoes, and hats with brims. The black asphalt park road in front of the lodge was just gravel with 1930s era cars parked up and down it. A Fred Harvey tour car zipped by loaded with tourists. The metallic sound of hammers pounding nails and the zip-zap of saws gnawing through wood boards filled my ears. Men wearing work overalls were scattered all around the unfinished log frame structure of Bright Angel Lodge. Neatly stacked piles of lumber were scattered around the building. A team of stone workers placed brick-sized rocks onto a layer of wet cement over top of a previous layer of rocks, slowly building the rock front of the lodge.

A woman with a large rolled-up piece of paper tucked under her arm walked through the construction site inspecting everyone's work. She paused in front of the building and spoke with a man who appeared to be the construction supervisor, pulling the paper out from under her arm and unrolling it. The man held one end and the woman held the other while she pointed to the design drawn on it and discussed building plans.

"Bright Angel Lodge started off with cabins and tents in 1885. Then Fred Harvey asked Mary Colter to renovate it for the growing number of tourists. Mary included one of the original cabins in her design: The Buckey O'Neill Cabin. Buckey O'Neill was one of Teddy Roosevelt's famous Rough Riders. He was an accomplished man. He was a newspaper reporter, a sheriff, a judge, a lawyer, and a mayor. He was killed in action in Cuba. Mary had a reputation for incorporating local materials and history in her designs. It was built in 1935. Let's get a closer look," Papa Lewis said.

We walked between piles of lumber and stone until we reached the front of the lodge. We were just feet away from Mary Colter herself! We could hear her tell the construction foreman that she was pleased with the rustic look of the front of the building. A man wearing an official National Park Service uniform emerged from the front door of the lodge and walked over to Mary and the foreman. His name tag identified him as Edwin McKee, Chief Naturalist.

"Excuse me, Ms. Colter," he interjected. "Would you like to see your completed geologic fireplace? All the stones that we cut from each layer of Grand Canyon were hauled up by mules this week and the stoneworkers did a great job."

"That's the park naturalist that worked with Mary Colter to layer the fireplace's stone to match the rock layers of Grand Canyon," Papa Lewis whispered to us.

"What's a geologic fireplace?" Hug-a-Bug whispered back to him.

Mary Colter overheard Hug-a-Bug's question. "Young lady, you and your family are welcome to come in and see it for yourself," she said, nodding to us in greeting.

"Thank you, ma'am. That would be mighty fine," Hug-a-Bug said, carefully choosing her words to sound like a girl from 1935.

We followed Mary Colter and the chief naturalist into the lodge. They led us past the limestone fireplace in the lobby and into the lounge area. Everyone there seemed to be taking a moment to stop in front of a fireplace on the back wall of the lodge. The outline of the fireplace's stone resembled the fluted shape of Grand Canyon.

"Young lady," Mary Colter began, motioning to Hug-a-Bug, "these rocks were carefully stacked to scientifically match the rocks in Grand Canyon. Down here on the hearth are river rocks you'll see along the Colorado River. The oldest rocks, the basement layer of Grand Canyon, we used for the first layer of stone on the fireplace. Each layer of this fireplace matches the layers of rocks by age in Grand Canyon along the Bright Angel Trail just like you would find hiking from the Colorado River all the way up to the rim."

"Ms. Colter, your work is amazing!" Hug-a-Bug exclaimed.

"Thank you, young lady, I'm glad you like it. I like my buildings to blend into their environment and include materials from their surroundings. Layering the stone of this fireplace to match Grand Canyon's layers seemed only natural," Mary answered.

We thanked Mary for allowing us to take a look at her latest project and then we exited the building, walking back to the same spot we time-traveled from. Everybody held hands and I said, "Take us back to the present."

Everything went dark, an invisible force pushed on

me, and then it was light again. Our clothes were back to our modern wicking outdoor wear. Papa Lewis led us back inside the lodge to the history room and Hug-a-Bug immediately rushed over to the geologic fireplace.

"This is so cool! After learning about how old some of the rocks are in Grand Canyon, and then meeting Mary Colter in person, I understand how perfect her geologic fireplace really is. This is a scientific work of art!" Hug-a-Bug declared. "I hope I'm as talented as her in my career."

"Me, too," I said. "She's so creative!"

"You're both already very talented," Papa Lewis assured us with a chuckle. "I knew you would enjoy learning about Mary Colter's work. She designed several more structures here, so we'll be seeing a lot more of what she's done. There's more to explore here in the history room, but we've got other things to do. We'll come back and check out the rest of this later. Right now, we should discuss our urgent matter."

I knew Papa Lewis wanted an update on our mission; I was surprised he even took the time to share the history of Mary Colter before asking me about it! But going to the history room was a nice reminder that we could enjoy the canyon's rich history while we were here on important business.

We followed Papa Lewis out of the Bright Angel Lodge. He led us along the Rim Trail toward the El Tovar Hotel. We all kept quiet about mission business until we were inside Mom and Dad's room and the door was safely shut.

CHAPTER 8

A New Plan

"I've been in contact with our extended time-traveling family in Acadia. Indeed, Arthur is the one who helped Branson with his geology presentation. Arthur is involved in a program for students to collaborate with other students around the country on national-park-related topics. Branson is in the same program and they worked on a geology project together," Papa Lewis explained.

For those of you who didn't read our Acadia National Park adventure, Arthur has the magical ability to time travel using an antique watch.

"Have you heard anything important from Blaze and Song? Do you know if they have the missing telescope lens?" Papa Lewis asked.

There was a knock at the door and we all froze.

"That's probably T2 and Sydney. We made plans to meet here to go over everything," Dad explained as he walked over and looked through the peephole before opening the door. T2 and Sydney walked in, zipping past everyone to join Hug-a-Bug and me on the couch.

"Well, any luck? Do they have the lens?" T2 asked us, eagerness in his voice.

"We know someone has the ability to time travel and they've been using it," I answered, looking at Hug-a-Bug, who shrugged. "We're not sure if it's Blaze and Song, though. While we were on the Trail of Time with the students today, Hug-a-Bug and I decided to take a swim in the ancient ocean that once existed where Grand Canyon is now 270 million years ago. While we were taking our ancient dip, a flash lit up the sky and we could hear faint voices. But we couldn't see anyone and couldn't identify the voices. One thing was for sure: they were definitely time travelers. We didn't want to blow our cover so we hid underwater for as long as we could to prevent being seen. When we came up for air, we could still hear faint voices, but we never saw anyone. But what we heard frightened us."

"What did you hear?" Papa Lewis asked.

"We heard one of the voices ask if this time travel could stop the formation of Grand Canyon," Hug-a-Bug replied.

I continued. "Then, there was a flash of bright light and an invisible force that pushed us underwater for a few seconds and the voices were gone. We swam to shore, traveled back to the present, and tried to identify if anyone from our adventure group seemed like they'd just dabbled in time travel. But no one seemed to be acting suspicious. Later though, at the end of our walk on the Trail of Time, we all explored the Yavapai Geology Museum. While we were inside the museum, Blaze, Song, and Branson disappeared. We found them all together along the Trail of Time, and Branson asked us if we could really go back in time and witness the Colorado River make Grand Canyon. Then he asked what would happen if something stopped Grand Canyon from forming. This all seemed suspicious, as if Branson knows we really can time travel."

"Could our magic time travel be used to stop the formation of Grand Canyon? Why would anyone want to do that?" Hug-a-Bug asked.

"This is precisely why we have measures in place to protect our time travel from landing in the wrong hands," Papa Lewis muttered, shaking his head. "This is also why your mission to get that missing lens back is so important."

"Hug-a-Bug, I don't think that the time travel magic alone could alter the creation of Grand Canyon. But someone with some engineering skills could change the flow of the Colorado River. If the flow of the river was altered during the creation of Grand Canyon, it could possibly impact the way the present-day Grand Canyon looks," T2 posed.

"How do you change the flow of a river?" Hug-a-Bug wondered aloud.

I knew exactly how. "You build a dam. There are lots of dams along the Colorado River. I read about two of them that are close by, the Hoover Dam downstream from Grand Canyon National Park and the Glen Canyon Dam upstream. Dams flood the area upriver and limit the flow of water downstream."

"Seriously Bubba Jones, do you really think a few kids with time travel magic could go back in time and construct something that would take thousands of people, engineering expertise, tons of cement, and years to build? I read about those dams, too," Hug-a-Bug countered.

"Actually, Bubba Jones is onto something," Papa Lewis reasoned. "A beaver can flood an entire area and choke off the flow of a river with just sticks and logs. But I don't think anyone's tried to disrupt the Colorado River since Grand Canyon is still here. Let's solve this mystery before something bad does happen, though."

"Song and Blaze love this park. They've grown up here. I know they would never want to harm this place's natural beauty. Maybe there is someone else involved? Maybe they weren't serious about preventing Grand Canyon from forming, they were just wondering about it," T2 added.

"We've enjoyed getting to know Blaze and Song," Hug-a-Bug told him, and he smiled as she went on. "They're so nice and fun and we like a lot of the same things. I only wish we could share our mission with them. They're family after all. Why don't we just ask them if they have the lens?" Hug-a-Bug said.

T2 patted Hug-a-Bug on the back. "I like your way of thinking, Hug-a-Bug, and I have good news. I volunteered to help chaperone your group on your backpacking adventure down to Phantom Ranch, and from what I understand, your Papa Lewis and your parents have agreed to help out, too."

"My knee's been giving me problems," Grandma Lewis said, and Hug-a-Bug rushed over to give her a hug. "I'll take a mule ride down, oh dear, your hugs always make me feel better! Mule rides usually book up a year in advance, but I got lucky and someone cancelled."

Sydney looked at T2 and smiled. "Song and Blaze will get to meet everyone tomorrow. Since they already know about our family's time travel powers, they'll realize that you're also time travelers when we tell them you're part of our family, and maybe then they'll share what happened to the missing lens, if they even know themselves! Either way, I think this is the best way to handle this situation until we find out more."

"I like this plan," Hug-a-Bug commented.

"Me, too," said Grandma Lewis, and Hug-a-Bug giggled.

I turned to T2. "So, can Hug-a-Bug and I just ask Blaze and Song if they have the lens?" I pleaded. "What do we have to lose? If they know we're relatives, hopefully they'll trust us."

"You bring up a good point. Even though recovering our time travel lens is very important and we must use spycraft to protect our magic, being honest with each other as family is a value we should always maintain," T2 concluded. "Yes, you can ask them."

"I'll send a message to Blaze and Song with an authentication code," Sydney said to us, thinking out loud. "I'll let them know that if they are approached by someone about our secret time travel magic, they should use the authentication code, and if the person answers them correctly, they should trust them." She thought for a moment, then continued. "They will say 'spaghetti' and you will respond with 'bat.' Okay?"

"Got it," I confirmed, and Hug-a-Bug gave Sydney a thumbs-up.

"Great! Since we have our plans set for tomorrow, shall we explore some more of the South Rim?" Papa Lewis suggested.

Hug-a-Bug and I told Papa Lewis how we walked past the Hopi House and Verkamp's Visitor Center today but didn't get a chance to check them out. He agreed that these are must-see attractions and we'd visit them next! We said goodbye to T2 and Sydney and marched out of the El Tovar Hotel over to the Hopi House.

"We learned from Tony and Harper that the Hopi House was designed by Ms. Colter to look like a Hopi pueblo," I said to Papa Lewis.

"The Hopi are descendants of the Ancestral Puebloans and are one of several tribes that call Grand Canyon home," Papa Lewis explained. "Mary Colter wanted the Hopi House to look like part of Old Oraibi, a Hopi village that dates back to approximately 1000 AD and is one of the oldest continuously inhabited villages in the United States. To make sure the building would be as authentic as possible, she hired Hopi people to construct it. Everything about Ms. Colter's design is authentic, except the doors. Hopi pueblos are typically entered from the roof, not ideal when your pueblo is expecting a regular flood of national park visitors. Let's go inside!"

We entered the building and Papa Lewis pointed out the stick ceiling laid over log beams and packed with mud. Like we'd heard from Tony and Harper, the Hopi House is a souvenir shop that sells items crafted by Native American artisans. Handmade blankets, handwoven baskets, and an assortment of jewelry were displayed on both levels of the building.

"A Hopi family once lived in the upper level of the Hopi House and would show various ritual dances to park visitors," Papa Lewis explained as we made our way to the upper level.

The skill of the Hopi who built this building and Mary Colter's attention to detail made us feel like we were inside an authentic Hopi pueblo. After we saw everything we could possibly see, marveling over all the amazing craftsmanship on display, we exited the Hopi House and followed Papa Lewis next door to Verkamp's Visitor Center.

"Before this was a national park, John Verkamp built

this building to sell items to tourists. Several generations of his family continued to operate this store for over a hundred years until they decided to discontinue it. In 2008, the National Park Service turned it into a visitor center and bookstore," Papa Lewis told us all as we walked towards the entrance.

The visitor center was jam-packed with interactive exhibits and tourists. We followed a historical timeline on the floor that highlighted various milestones in park history as well as U.S. history. A replica of John Verkamp's first Grand Canyon retail operation, a simple canvas tent, included descriptions of how this business began and changed through the years.

From there, Papa Lewis led us on a short stroll along the Rim Trail back towards the Bright Angel Lodge to a sign that read "Lookout Studio." Perched on the very edge of the Grand Canyon Rim was a stone building that looked almost as if it was a natural extension of the rock surrounding it. The building had an enclosed observation area and an open outdoor observation area.

"Lookout Studio, also called 'The Lookout,' was built by guess who, Hug-a-Bug?" Papa Lewis asked.

"Mary Colter! She sure had an eye for design," Hug-a-Bug answered as we walked through the multi-level building up to an enclosed observation tower.

"The building looks the same as it did when it was built in 1914," Papa Lewis added.

"How would you know? Oh wait, never mind," I teased.

We left the building and stood along the outside observation area, gazing out at the gorgeous Grand Canyon.

"There are many more adventures to have, but now you two need to get back to the school group for a good night's sleep. We have a big day tomorrow," Papa Lewis reminded us.

"I dropped your backpacks off at your lodge so you can pack up for our overnight trip to the bottom of Grand Canyon tomorrow," Dad added.

"Thanks, Dad." I hugged him, and he gave me a big squeeze.

Papa Lewis, Grandma, Dad, and Mom walked with us until we reached the back entrance to the Bright Angel Lodge, where the school adventure group was staying. Hug-a-Bug and I made sure we'd hugged everyone good-night before we went inside.

CHAPTER 9

RELATIVES, LEGENDS, & FACTS

It was dinner time for the Adventure Club! A sign posted on the wall in the lobby read "Adventure Club Dinner in the Restaurant," and thanks to that and several other helpful signs with arrows, we were guided to our group.

Large chandeliers filled the dining room with light and we quickly spotted our adventure group seated at two large rectangular tables. Tony and Harper were standing and speaking to the group as we walked in. Hug-a-Bug and I quietly sat down at one of the tables next to Blaze and Song; they'd saved us seats! Clean place settings were neatly arranged in front of everyone.

"We secured your backpacks in our lodge rooms, and we'll fill you in on the preparations we did while you were gone," Blaze whispered to Hug-a-Bug and me, trying not to interrupt Tony and Harper.

"Thanks," I said, and he smiled.

We submitted our food orders when we signed up for the Adventure Club, so we didn't have to worry about meals. Servers approached our table and gave everyone a dinner plate with a burger and a large salad. Harper and Tony wrapped up their discussion about the hike and everyone grew silent as they ate, chatting more and more the fuller we became. Then we walked with Blaze and Song back to our rooms to prepare our gear for the morning hike.

The four of us decided to stick together and hang out in Song and Hug-a-Bug's room. "Here's your gear," Song said to Hug-a-Bug and I, pointing to our backpacks and hiking poles.

"Thank you for helping us with our gear, Song," I said.

"That's what friends are for," she said, grinning.

"Actually, all of us are more than just friends," Hug-a-Bug commented, glancing between all of us.

Blaze raised an eyebrow. "Huh? What do you mean?"

"We're here with our Papa Lewis, Grandma Lewis, my mom, and my dad. T2 picked us up the other day in his helicopter. Our Papa Lewis and T2 have been on national park adventures together, because T2 is a relative of ours," I explained carefully, leaving out the magical time travel connection.

Blaze and Song looked at each other, surprised. "Uncle T2 and Aunt Sydney adopted us," Song said slowly. "When you say you're related to T2, how are you related?"

"Well, according to legend, our family inherited a unique *skill* that dates back to the Lewis and Clark expedition. T2 and Papa Lewis are both part of that family, direct descendants," I explained, waiting.

Blaze nudged Song. "These legendary skills you mentioned," she said, twisting a strand of her hair around her finger, "do they have anything to do with…time?"

I nodded. Hug-a-Bug, much more to-the-point, said, "Yes, time *and* travel to be exact!"

Blaze's eyes widened. "Spaghetti," he said.

The authentication message! It was good to see that Blaze and Song were practicing protocol.

"Bat," Hug-a-Bug responded. And with that, the twins visibly relaxed.

"What do you know about time travel?" Blaze immediately asked.

"We're time travelers! I inherited the ability from Papa Lewis and Hug-a-Bug will soon have the ability as well. I can take anyone back in time if they're within ten feet of me," I answered.

Blaze didn't miss a beat. "Do you need an object to time travel?"

I ripped the Velcro fasteners of my cargo pocket open and removed my time travel journal. "Yes, this is my time travel tool. This journal dates all the way back to the Lewis and Clark expedition. It has been handed down through the generations. Just like your family's time travel telescope."

"So you already know about T2's magical telescope?" Song asked.

Hug-a-Bug nodded and I spoke. "We sure do! Do you have it with you?" This was it, the moment that could solve our mystery.

Song looked over at Blaze. "I'll explain," he said to her before turning back to me. "It's more complicated than a telescope," he began. "Just before we left for Grand Canyon Adventure Camp, T2 and Sydney took us on our own little adventure in the park. On our return from a day hike, we stopped in Kolb Studio to have a look around. When we got to the residence area, there was a tripod-mounted telescope near a window, and what happened next completely amazed us."

"What's the Kolb Studio?" Hug-a-Bug interjected.

"It's a multi-storied home built right on the edge of the South Rim, just steps from our room here," Song explained.

"We were just at the Lookout Studio; how did we miss this?" I asked.

"Kolb Studio is to the west of Lookout Studio; along the Rim Trail, just past Lookout Studio. The Kolb brothers had a photography business in the early days of tourism to Grand Canyon. They would photograph tourists as they rode mules down into the canyon," Blaze explained. "When the tourists returned to the rim, the

Kolb brothers would sell them their picture as a keepsake. Now with smartphones and digital cameras, taking someone's picture is no big deal. But these guys were doing this as early as 1901 using practically ancient camera equipment by today's standards. Back then, you needed water to develop your film. So they had to run down the trail to Indian Garden to a spring to process their film and hurry back to the trailhead to sell the photographs in time. The spring was over nine miles round trip. To get attention and grow their business, these guys would stage death-defying shots to sell pictures. One of their most famous exploits was when they filmed a motion picture of their boat retracing Major John Wesley Powell's journey down the Colorado River. They showed that film in the studio to tourists. It is the longest running movie in existence."

"It sounds like these guys had a pretty fun and adventurous way of making a living," I commented.

"Yeah, they sure did," Blaze agreed. "But anyway, T2 said that his dad knew Emery Kolb and would take him to the studio to hear Emory's lectures and watch his film when he was a kid. Then T2 began to tell us about his time travel magic. That's when it happened. He reached into his daypack and removed an old telescope. The telescope looked like something you would see a pirate using to navigate the high seas, which is pretty cool. But the next thing we knew, we were back in 1915, sitting in the Kolb auditorium! The room was filled with people, and we all listened to Emery Kolb's lecture and watched his 1911 river trip film. Then T2 seamlessly brought us back to the present. Song and I were completely confused by what just happened, and then we heard a group of tourists approach as part of a guided tour through Kolb Studio, and T2 crammed the telescope into my backpack so we wouldn't look suspicious. After the group moved on to another room, we left the Kolb Studio and T2 told us about the importance of keeping this time travel magic secret and he taught us how to communicate using codes like spies do."

"Hug-a-Bug and I felt exactly the same way when our Papa Lewis took us back for the first time. How often do you go back in time?" I asked.

"Well, here's the thing: I completely forgot the telescope was in my backpack and we continued to explore the park that day." Blaze sighed. "If I'd remembered that the telescope was still in my bag, I'd have probably been more careful. But I was rough with my pack. I tossed it on the ground when we took breaks, threw it in the trunk of the car, used it as a seat sometimes even. It was late when we got home that evening and T2 asked me to put the telescope back in his backpack, which I did, but apparently the lens part of the telescope popped out and remained in my daypack, probably because of all the jostling. But I didn't realize this until we were on the Trail of Time earlier today.

"When I assembled my day pack with water and snacks for this trip, I didn't even notice the lens. Then, you guys disappeared near where we learned about the ancient sea. The group moved on, but Tony and Harper noticed after a bit that you were gone and assumed you guys slipped off to use the restroom, so they told Branson to pause and let everyone take a break. But I knew there wasn't a restroom near where we saw you both last. So, while the group lounged around sipping water and eating snacks, Song and I backtracked to look for you. For some reason, Branson followed us. And as I stood there wondering where you guys went, I imagined what it would've been like to swim in that ancient sea. And all of the sudden, I felt like I was having an out of body experience! I could see the ancient ocean, but I was still here in the present. I felt like I was in a dream. I think I even saw you and Hug-a-Bug swimming. It was all so weird. But when I found the lens in my daypack, it all made sense."

Hug-a-Bug gasped. "We heard voices while we were swimming, but we never saw anyone. That explains why," she said. "Before we knew about the time travel magic, whenever Papa Lewis would tell us a story about one of his adventures, it just felt to us like we were there with him, like we were imagining it all or something. We didn't physically leave the present, but we could actually see the place back in time that Papa Lewis was talking about. I just thought it was because Papa Lewis was such a good storyteller. But, after Papa Lewis let us in on the magical secret, he explained that in order to *physically* go back in time, you need to actually *speak it,* like say the 'when' you're going to while understanding exactly what the magic can do. If you just imagine a past event when you have our journal or your lens, you don't fully time travel; your mind just goes into a dreamlike state and you can kinda *see* the past, while your body remains in the present, and those within a very close radius may experience what you're experiencing. Papa Lewis warned us that this can be dangerous if you're driving a car or doing something that requires you to focus. But, it's a nifty time travel tool that can be used to quickly flip through the past inconspicuously. Apparently, based on our ancient lake experience, your voices from the present were able to transmit to the past, even when you were physically in the present. Amazing!"

"And that was Hug-a-Bug and I swimming in the ancient ocean," I added. "We tried to hide, but apparently, it didn't work. We like to hit all the ancient swimming holes. It's a time travel perk."

Song shrugged. "I don't blame you."

"Do you still have the telescope lens?" I asked.

Blaze shook his head. "We don't, and that's what has Song and me worried. Uncle T2 and Aunt Sydney have been so good to us. We lost our parents, but Uncle T2 and Aunt Sydney took us in. Then they tell us about this time travel magic! Who would have ever imagined you could time travel? We're excited to become part of the family mission to protect and preserve our natural wildlands." He paused, lowering his head. "But now we've let T2 down."

Hug-a-Bug placed a hand on his shoulder. "Don't blame yourself," she said. "This whole thing was a total accident.

We'll help you find the lens. That's why we're here."

"Are you serious?" Song asked.

"Absolutely," I confirmed. "We're going to get that lens back. Word spreads fast in our time travel family when something happens to the magic. It's our responsibility to help each other."

"So, let's start with where and when you last had the telescope lens," Hug-a-Bug suggested.

Blaze blushed, clearly embarrassed. "After that episode where we saw you guys swimming in the ancient ocean, I panicked! I knew immediately that this time travel magic probably had something to do with what had happened, but I didn't know what to do. Like you just explained, it wasn't like when Uncle T2 showed the magic to us; he'd specifically say a time that we went to, and then we'd be there. But we realized that whoever was near us on the hike might also experience a dreamlike view of any period I happened to think about! I remembered that I had given Uncle T2 his telescope back, but to be sure I dumped my pack out and there it was: the telescope lens. I tried to be calm, but all I could think about was how much I'd just put our family's magic in danger, how many people I might've accidentally taken back and forth in time! We were coming up on the Jurassic period, and I didn't want to chance going back to when there were *dinosaurs*! I stepped off the trail and tucked the lens beneath a branch hidden by a rock. Someone must have watched me do it because when I went back to retrieve the lens, it was gone." He shook his head. "I shouldn't have left it out there, that was so *stupid* of me—"

"Don't be so hard on yourself," I interrupted, meeting his eyes. "You were in a tough situation and you panicked, it happens."

"Who saw the ancient ocean with you besides Song? Do you know?" Hug-a-Bug asked.

"Branson for sure, because he followed us and described the same ancient lake experience as us. No one else said anything and Branson was the only person near us when that happened. But I don't think Branson knew about our time traveling ability before it happened."

"Who in the group suggested going back to stop Grand Canyon from forming?" I asked.

"Branson said that a few times," Blaze admitted. "But I don't think he was serious. I mean how could one guy stop Grand Canyon from forming? We didn't take him seriously. It was odd though that when we were all getting ready to board the bus today, I found Branson along the Trail of Time, at the exact point in the timeline where the Colorado River began to form Grand Canyon. I told Song to hurry back to where I stashed the lens to retrieve it before we boarded the bus. That's when we realized the lens was missing."

"How well do you know Branson?"

"We met him for the first time in Williamson for this Adventure Camp."

Hug-a-Bug looked confused. "You mean he doesn't go to your school?"

"Nope. Tony introduced him to us and said that he

was going to lead a special 'time travel' presentation," Blaze answered.

"Did anybody else arrive in the park with him?" I asked.

"I'm not sure. Tony might be able to answer that," Blaze replied.

"So, Branson is an unknown transplant. No one knew him until he showed up at this Adventure Camp with a prearranged time travel project. He's curious about stopping the formation of Grand Canyon. The lens that you stashed is missing and the only person from Adventure Camp who was on the Trail of Time when you went to get the lens was Branson," Hug-a-Bug summarized. She looked in turn at each of us. "Sounds like he's our culprit."

CHAPTER 10

A Knock on Buckey's Door

"What should we do?" Song asked, her eyes wide.

"Do you know where Branson's room is? Maybe we could pay him a visit," I suggested. "If he doesn't know we're coming and he has the lens, we might have a chance to at least confirm he has it."

Blaze nodded. "Sounds like a good plan to me. He's in the Buckey O'Neill cabin. Since he shared his whole presentation with us, they honored him by providing him with the most historical room at Bright Angel's Lodge. Let's go."

Blaze led the way and we followed him out of the

lodge and along the Rim Trail.

"Why is the Buckey O'Neill cabin the most historical?" I asked.

"William 'Buckey' O'Neill built himself a cabin here in the 1890s before Bright Angel Lodge existed," Song responded. "Buckey played a key role in the development of the park. He convinced the Santa Fe Railway to run a train line to Grand Canyon. He never got to see it happen though, because he volunteered as a Teddy Roosevelt Rough Rider in the Spanish American War and he was killed in action in Cuba."

We all quietly thought about that. "That's so sad," Hug-a-Bug said, and Song nodded.

"Yes, it was unfortunate," Blaze agreed. "I've always wanted to see the inside of the Buckey O'Neill cabin, and I guess this is my chance. And, um, since I messed up so much before, I need to make up for it. I'm going to do everything I can to get this lens back. So, guys, I'll handle this. Let me do the talking."

I shrugged. "You've got it, Blaze. If you need help, we're right here with you."

In under a minute we came upon the one-story log cabin with a stone chimney and two side-by-side front doors, perched just feet from the rim of Grand Canyon. It was nestled in among several other cabins, but its rustic exterior definitely stood out.

Blaze knocked on the door. Moments later it cracked open, and Branson peered through the opening.

"Hey, Branson. Sorry to bother you, but can we talk

to you a minute?" Blaze asked. I'd thought he might be a bit nervous about all this, but he seemed very calm and composed. I was proud of him. It's not easy to push on after you've made a mistake.

"Sure. What's up?" Branson replied as he stepped outside and closed the door.

Blaze didn't skip a beat. "Actually, can we step in? I've always wanted to see Buckey's cabin, and you're the first person I've ever known that's actually staying here."

Branson didn't seem to suspect anything. "Um, well, I guess that's okay. Give me a minute though, alright?" There was some hesitation in his voice as he dashed back into his two-room suite and disappeared into the far room.

We stepped inside and stayed near the door. Branson's hiking gear was strewn everywhere just like ours was; everyone was preparing for our big hike in the morning. I'd barely started glancing around for the lens when Branson reappeared from the other room.

"This cabin is nice. It's hard to believe that it's the oldest building here in the park. Okay, so anyway, what's up?" Branson said as he joined us.

"Are you staying here by yourself?" I asked. "It is pretty big for one person."

"Yeah it is, and it'll just be me. My dad's in the park though, and he may drop by tonight to check on me."

"Where are you from?" Hug-a-Bug asked.

"Flagstaff, not too far from here."

Blaze swallowed once, gathering his courage. "Branson,

earlier today did you happen to find a loose telescope lens along the Trail of Time? I took it out of my backpack on the trail and lost it and I need to get it back. It's very important to me."

Branson answered quickly and defensively. "Why do you think I have it? What would I do with a loose telescope lens?"

"You were the only one in our group that went back out to the Trail of Time besides us after your presentation ended. We just wanted to be sure you didn't pick it up and bring it to a lost and found or something," Hug-a-Bug responded. "If it wasn't you who found it, somebody outside of our group might've stolen it. We might have to file a theft report."

Branson scoffed. "Theft report?! Do you really think someone would steal just a lens? No one would even know what it was when they first saw it! Just let it go; you can always buy a new one or something."

Song, Hug-a-Bug, Blaze, and I looked at each other, then back at Branson. "That's a good point, Branson," Blaze said curtly. "We'll let you get back to packing; sorry to bother you."

"Yeah, sure, whatever, no worries," Branson said, relaxing a little. His eyes brightened. "Just think though, tomorrow we're going to walk through time again as we descend into Grand Canyon."

We told him how excited we were for tomorrow and said goodnight, filing out of Buckey's historic cabin. As soon as Branson shut the door, Blaze sighed. "He has to have it. He got so defensive in there. I bet he hid it."

"He's not going to just let us go through his stuff," Song pointed out. "We need a better way to confirm he has the lens and get it back."

"Maybe I can try to take us back in time and the lens will take us there. That means it's definitely in there somewhere," Blaze said, his eyes bright. We moved around to a side of the cabin away from windows and checked to make sure no one was watching us. Blaze closed his eyes and muttered, "Take us back to meet Buckey at his cabin. Take us back."

We huddled near him and waited for something to happen. Nothing did.

Blaze clenched his teeth. "Urgh, dang it! It's hopeless!"

I put an arm around his shoulders. "It was a good idea, Blaze, but it just might not work right now. We might not be close enough. But we could try again on the trail during our trip to confirm the lens's location." He seemed a little less resigned, and I wanted to keep encouraging him, but it was getting late. "Hug-a-Bug and I need to get our gear ready for tomorrow, okay? Don't worry, this search isn't over yet."

"Well, Bubba, maybe we should do one more thing for Blaze and Song before we pack our stuff," Hug-a-Bug suggested, nudging me with her arm. "Since we're already here and all."

Blaze's eyes widened as he realized what Hug-a-Bug was suggesting, and Song gasped and smiled. "You guys don't have to do that!" she said, but I'd already made my decision, pulling us all close together for the trip.

I placed my hand on my magic journal. "Take us back to 1898 to meet Buckey."

A sudden wind whipped up and pushed against us. Then everything went quiet. The exterior lights of the Bright Angel Lodge were gone, because the whole lodge was gone. Silver moonlight illuminated Buckey's cabin. The windows glowed golden from the kerosene lamps inside. Our clothing had transformed. Blaze and I wore long pants held up with suspenders, cowboy boots, and wide-brimmed hats. Hug-a-Bug and Song now wore long ankle-length dresses, brimmed hats, and leather shoes.

A man stepped out of the front door of the cabin and walked to the very edge of the rim. He gazed out across Grand Canyon, clearly savoring the silvered view. We could see him well even in just the moonlight. He had dark hair and a mustache, and there was a pistol in the holster at his waist. A woman stepped out of the cabin and joined the man, and they both stood together in tranquil silence. We ducked behind some Ponderosa pines to stay out of sight.

"Wow, this is awesome. That's Buckey and his wife," Blaze whispered, barely containing his excitement.

We could hear Buckey speaking to his wife just then. "I sure will miss you and this view we have here. But I need to do my duty. I'm going with the Rough Riders to Cuba. When I get back, hopefully we can get the Santa Fe Railroad to lay some track from here to Williams. Train service would help draw tourists and miners to the area."

Blaze shook his head. "What a bummer. Buckey will never get to witness the railroad line from Williams to here. He was killed in action in Cuba. The railroad he fought so hard for was a huge success and is still in service today."

"He left a nice life here with a home that overlooked the amazing Grand Canyon to volunteer to serve his country, and he never made it back," I whispered with sadness.

We quietly slipped further back from the rim and formed a circle. I said, "Take us back to the present."

A gust of wind pushed hard against us. Everything went dark, and then the area was illuminated once again by the exterior lights from the Bright Angel Lodge. We all wore our modern clothes again. Buckey's cabin was nestled in with several other newer cabins along the rim.

"I think it's cool that Mary Colter preserved Buckey's cabin and included it in her design plans for Bright Angel Lodge," Hug-a-Bug said.

"Wow, Bubba Jones, thank you for bringing us back to see Buckey. You time-traveled like a pro, just like T2 showed us," Blaze said.

I smiled at him. "No worries. And we'll do our best to get that lens back tomorrow."

We strolled back to our rooms, finished packing our gear, and slipped into bed, and I fell asleep as soon as my head hit the pillow. I woke up in the morning to a knock on the door followed by the familiar voices of Tony and Harper.

"Wake up, breakfast in 30 minutes! Let's go!"

CHAPTER 11

TAIL OF TWO SQUIRRELS

This would be an exciting day. Ever since I heard about Papa Lewis's adventures in Grand Canyon, I have always wanted to hike down to the Colorado River from the rim, and today we were going to do just that. I also hoped that we could solve the missing-lens mystery and successfully help our family!

The Adventure Club gathered in the restaurant for breakfast. Then we returned to our rooms, grabbed our gear, and assembled in the lobby. Tony and Harper led us through the front doors and out of the lodge. We walked along the Village Loop Drive and made a right just past the train depot, pushing on until we reached the Backcountry Information Center. Inside were two park rangers who were busy reviewing maps and permits with a group of hikers at the counter. We set our packs down while Tony and Harper waited in line to review our overnight group camping permit. The door swung open and in walked T2, Papa Lewis, and Dad. They each shouldered backpacks and carried trekking poles. T2 introduced Papa Lewis and Clark to Blaze and Song.

"We have two famous adventurers joining us on our hike," he told them with a grin. "I want to introduce you both to Lewis and Clark, not to be confused with the original Lewis and Clark from the Corps of Discovery expedition."

"I'm Blaze; it's nice to meet you both. Pretty cool that you're named after Lewis and Clark," Blaze said.

"Nice to meet you! I'm Song." Song held out her hand to shake.

"We are family, Miss Song," Papa Lewis said, opening his arms. "You can have a hug if you want one."

Song smiled and gave him a hug, as did Blaze, and Hug-a-Bug and I both gave our Dad a squeeze, which made him laugh.

"The ladies decided to join your grandma on her mule ride down to Phantom Ranch. They got lucky; their names were on a waiting list and two more mules became available and a room opened at the ranch that could accommodate all of them. We'll stop by and say hi to them later today," Dad explained.

Harper and Tony introduced T2, Papa Lewis, and

our dad to the rest of the group and explained that they were seasoned outdoorsman and would accompany our group as chaperones. We all filed outside and waited for the park shuttle bus. Minutes later, we were all on board and en route to the main visitor center. From there, we switched to the orange bus which would take us to our trailhead, the South Kaibab Trail. The shuttle buses were a really convenient way to get around the park, and we didn't have to pay for them; they're free.

Our bus wound down Desert View Drive. Grand Canyon to our left was camouflaged by the towering Ponderosa pines and Gambel oak trees. We had been so focused on the rocks and solving our mystery over the last few days that we hadn't really taken the time to notice all the amazing wildlife around us. Several deer grazed near the side of the road. They looked different from their whitetail cousins I was used to seeing back east. T2 saw Hug-a-Bug and I glued to our view out of the bus window and leaned over to us.

"Many first-time visitors don't think about the abundance of wildlife in Grand Canyon until they get here. Grand Canyon has several different climates and elevations which support a wide range of plants and wildlife. Those there are mule deer. They get their name from their big mule-like ears, and you'll notice that their tails are white with a black tip. They're native and are found in the many forest areas along the rim and even in the desert scrub areas down in the canyon. Now, the elk you see scattered among the trees, they are not indigenous. They were brought to Arizona in the early 1900s and migrated up from Williams. They've adapted to the Ponderosa pine forest and the Pinyon-juniper woodland down in the canyon and along the rim. Since elk are not native to this habitat, they have a hard time finding water and often use human water sources, which tends to cause dangerous human encounters. They have hurt people who've gotten too close. As a rule of thumb, keep your distance from any deer and elk, and honestly all wild animals for that matter. Both the mule deer and the elk are prey to mountain lions, bobcats, and coyotes."

"So, 'indigenous' means the same as 'native,' naturally occurring in a place?" Hug-a-Bug asked T2.

"You got that right," T2 confirmed.

"Did you say mountain lions?" I asked. "Don't they stalk their prey?"

"Yep, we're in mountain lion country. But you don't have to worry. They don't consider humans prey, although you shouldn't hike alone. Mountain lions are skillful hunters. They're like the Navy SEALs of wild creatures with their careful stealth as they hunt mule deer and elk. They wait for the perfect opportunity to pounce on their prey. They're nocturnal and can see very well at night."

"That's good that we're not considered prey at least," I replied.

"Grand Canyon is loaded with life," Song chimed in. "I just learned in school that there are 92 mammals, 447 types of birds, and 58 reptiles and amphibians here in Grand Canyon, not to mention all the plant life and thousands of invertebrate species."

"Wow!" Hug-a-Bug exclaimed. "That's a lot. What's an invertebrate?"

"All species that don't have a spinal backbone, like insects, spiders, worms, and scorpions, are called invertebrates," Song answered.

"Bison are another mammal you can see in Grand Canyon that aren't indigenous," T2 interjected. "There's a sizable herd on the North Rim, but none on the South Rim. They were brought here in the early 1900s and the herd has since expanded in size. The bison have impacted delicate forest meadows and various water sources, so park officials are working on ways to reduce the herd in the park."

"It's interesting how elk and bison have been welcomed in other national parks through reintroduction programs, but since they aren't indigenous to Grand Canyon and aren't necessarily helpful to the living diversity here, they aren't wanted," I summarized.

"Going to school here has helped me learn a lot about the local wildlife," said Blaze. "Every area has its own unique thing going for it. Like, see those squirrels zipping around in the trees?" Blaze pointed out the window at the forest, where there were indeed squirrels skittering across the trees' branches. "Those are tassel-eared squirrels. They feed on the Ponderosa pine trees and then kinda pay the trees back 'cause their scat is full of nutrients."

I raised an eyebrow. "Are you telling me that squirrel poop is *nutritious*?"

"Yep, for the Ponderosa pines anyway."

"That's gross!" Hug-a-Bug blurted out.

Blaze shrugged. "That's how the natural world works. But, there's also something else unique about the tassel-eared squirrel. The ones you see here on the South Rim are known as the Abert's squirrel. But the same species found on the North Rim is known as the Kaibab squirrel. Because the canyon separates the two groups, the Kaibab squirrel evolved to have a unique white tail unlike the Abert's squirrel,."

"Wow, that's cool!" I said.

Song thought for a moment, then smiled. "Hm, the cutest-looking animal here, I think, is the ringtail cat. Although, I've never seen one in the wild. It's the state mammal of Arizona. It has a black-and-white striped tail like a raccoon and its ears give it kind of a red-fox look. They're nocturnal, so they only come out at night."

The bus screeched to a halt and the driver announced, "South Kaibab Trail Head!"

Our group stood up from our seats and filed off the bus. Everyone extended their trekking poles and slipped their packs on. You could tell based on everyone's gear and how quickly they were ready to go that these were seasoned hikers. Tony and Harper unfolded their topography map and everyone gathered around them.

"The South Kaibab Trail will take us 6.4 miles down and is the most direct route to the Colorado River," Tony explained, sliding his finger along an orange-highlighted black-dotted line on his map.

"This trail is well-traveled," Harper continued. "It's part

of the 800-mile Arizona Trail that stretches from Mexico to Utah. It's also a popular route for those that walk from the South Rim to the North Rim or vice versa, who are known as 'rim to rim' hikers. Right now, though, the North Rim is encased in snow, so we shouldn't run into too many rim-to-rim hikers. A lot of day hikers also access this trail, and we'll be sharing the trail with mule teams, too. When we come upon a mule train, step to the inside of the trail away from the edge and remain quiet and calm so you don't spook any of the mules. Wait until the mule train is about fifty feet beyond us before making noise."

"When we get to the river, we'll have just a short distance to go before we reach our camp destination, the Bright Angel Campground, along Bright Angel Creek," Tony said, placing his finger on the map near Phantom Ranch.

"We'll take the Bright Angel Trail back up to the South Rim tomorrow," Harper explained, and Tony slid his finger along the dotted line marking the Bright Angel Trail. She continued. "Remember, we're descending down into the desert. Everyone, double-check your water. Do you have enough? This is your last chance for water until we get to our campsite. Also, make sure you've put on enough sunscreen. Do it now, before we get moving."

We all dug into our packs to do a last-minute check on our water, and applied a bit of extra sunscreen to our faces, making sure we were thorough and covered every corner and wrinkle.

Once everyone settled, Tony gave us all a thumbs-up. "It's time, guys," he said with a grin. "Let's go."

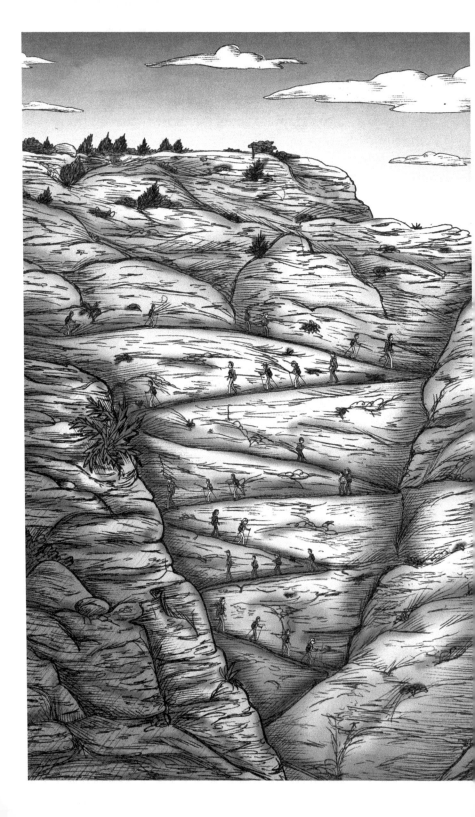

CHAPTER 12

WHAT GOES DOWN MUST COME UP!

We marched along a path toward the trailhead and we were rewarded with yet another amazing view of Grand Canyon. The sky was baby blue with perfect puffy white clouds floating overhead. You could see for miles across the red-tinted rock layers and down into the canyon gorge with its speckled terrain shrouded in desert scrub.

Our group descended single file onto the South Kaibab Trail. This trail was built by the National Park Service in 1925. Each step I took kicked up a cloud of red dust as we zig-zagged along, switching directions back and forth in an area known as the "Chimney." Thinking back to what we learned on the Trail of Time yesterday, we were now walking from the newest rock in Grand Canyon all the way down to the basement rock at the bottom.

"The trail guide said that each step down into the canyon takes you back in time 100,000 years. That's so amazing," Hug-a-Bug gushed.

Branson led the group with Tony and Harper. He had been strangely quiet all morning. Meanwhile Blaze, Song, Hug-a-Bug and I brought up the rear with T2, Papa Lewis, and Dad. The other kids in the group were sandwiched between us. It wasn't exactly the best positioning for our plan.

"Last month, the upper parts of this trail were covered in ice, but that's gone now. The North Rim is over 8,000 feet above sea level and is much colder and still blanketed with snow. The South Rim, where we started our hike from, is around 7,000 feet above sea level. The Paiute Native American Tribe call Grand Canyon 'Kaibab' which means 'mountain turned upside down,'" Blaze commented.

"Could you imagine snow in Grand Canyon? Sledding down trails like this?" Hug-a-Bug responded, grinning. "It would be extreme."

I smiled. It felt good to be on the trail with our new friends, especially knowing that Papa Lewis and Dad were nearby. We've been on so many adventures together and knowing they were here to help us solve this mystery provided some comfort. It was also nice to experience such an amazing park with family. As I walked along, my mind drifted to the missing lens. I wondered if Branson had it in his backpack right now, and how we were going to get Blaze closer to him so we could try out our plan.

After zipping back and forth for a while, everyone stopped at an amazing view, very different from what we'd seen before now that we were below the rim. We were at Ooh Aah Point and there was so much to see there that a camera couldn't capture it all in a single picture. Every pivot brought a newly stunning view. And everything felt very still, almost as if we were on an uninhabitable planet. The wind-worn rock told a story from every angle, one of steady and subtle change.

We continued along a ridge with breathtaking canyon views in all directions. We passed by Cedar Ridge, pushing on. In the heat of the summer, most day-hikers would turn back here to stay hydrated and safe from the intense heat. The lead hikers in our group stopped suddenly as a line of mules appeared on the trail in the distance. Several more mules appeared as they climbed up from the trail below. We all stepped aside and grew silent to let the mule train safely go by. Eight mules passed, each with a human in the saddle. The riders all wore smiles on their faces, wide-brimmed hats on their heads, and sunglasses over their eyes. After the mule train passed, we continued our descent.

We stopped for a rest at Skeleton Point. We took off our packs and sat down to sip on our water and break out some snacks. It was still late spring, and already it was very hot out. In another month, the heat down here would get so intense that it could be deadly. When the powerful summer heat kicks in, hiking is recommended in the early morning and late evening, and people are told to stay off the trail during the day. If you do hike in the summer daytime heat, park officials suggest not to attempt to go all the way down. We packed salty foods and sports drinks, both recommended for hiking in this hot climate.

While we sat on our packs, Blaze pulled out his binoculars and scanned the area. "Hey guys, have you ever seen desert bighorn sheep?" he asked as he glanced around.

"No? Do you see them? Where are they?" I asked.

"Heading in our direction from over there. It looks like a small herd," Blaze said as he handed me his binoculars and pointed towards the canyon ridge not far from where we sat.

I peered through his binoculars and immediately located several brown stout creatures with stocky bodies. Some of them had thick large horns and they curled around themselves almost forming a complete circle on either side of the head. These impressive animals walked effortlessly along a narrow steep canyon wall.

"That's so cool," I said. These desert bighorn sheep were close enough that we could see them even without binoculars, but everyone wanted to have a peek anyway. I handed the binoculars to Hug-a-Bug.

"The desert bighorn sheep is the largest indigenous

mammal in Grand Canyon. They travel in small herds. A male is called a ram and a female is called an ewe," Papa Lewis explained.

"To be able to walk along a canyon ridge like that, they must be some tough animals," I said.

While we were all watching the desert bighorn sheep, T2 had pulled out his magical telescope. He extended it out and held it up to his eye and pointed it out toward the sheep.

"Something is wrong with my telescope," he said, and pretty convincingly, too. "It's not helping with my view. I can see just as well without it. Look at that, the magnifying lens is missing." T2 pointed to the end of the telescope that was missing its lens, acting as if he just discovered it was gone.

Branson nearly choked on his energy bar and let out a gasping cough which convinced me he either had the missing telescope lens or he knew exactly who did! But what was T2 up to? Did he hope to flush out the lens with this act? We didn't have a chance to update him on what happened to the lens and everything else from last night. I decided to play along with T2's act.

"What happened to your telescope? How did you lose the lens?" I asked T2.

"I don't know, but I sure would like that lens back," T2 replied.

Tony came over to look at T2's telescope. "That looks like an antique. Where did you get it?"

"It's been handed down from one generation to the

next in our family for over 150 years. About the time of Powell's Colorado expedition, actually. It breaks my heart that the lens is missing," T2 responded.

"Wow, I sure hope you find it. That's an impressive piece of history, T2," Tony said.

"It sure is. Thanks, Tony."

"Uncle T2, we need to talk," Blaze murmured to his uncle.

"Sure, what's up?" T2 asked softly.

Blaze sighed. "I'll tell you later."

"I've got a telescope just like that," Branson suddenly said as he reached into his backpack and pulled out a telescope. He extended it to its full length and peered out at the desert bighorn sheep. "Mine works great."

"Can I see?" I asked Branson.

"I guess so, just be careful, it's an antique, too," Branson replied as he handed me his telescope.

I took a look through it. It had a lens in the end and worked just as a telescope should. But why did he also have a telescope like this? Did he place the missing lens in it? This all seemed rather strange. I didn't want to make a scene in front of the rest of the hikers about time travel, but we needed to get to the bottom of this soon.

Just then, Hug-a-Bug walked up and snatched Branson's telescope away from me. "Let me have a look," she insisted as she held the telescope up to her eye and then walked down the trail with it clutched in her hand.

"Hey, where did she go with my telescope?" Branson asked as he stood up, put away his water bottle, strapped on his pack, and headed down the trail after Hug-a-Bug.

Blaze, Song, and I quickly grabbed our things and hurried after them as fast as we could.

"Hey, guys, let's stick together as a group!" Harper yelled after us, but there was no turning back now. I felt bad that we were ditching the group, but we had a mission to complete. I could see Hug-a-Bug up in the distance, and Branson closing in on her from behind, followed by Blaze and Song. This was our chance to see if Branson had the missing magical lens.

I trekked as fast as I could and caught up with Blaze and Song. The three of us continued in pursuit of Branson and Hug-a-Bug, who were in sight but still out of reach up ahead in the distance. I felt powerless as I saw Branson catch up to Hug-a-Bug and grab the telescope from her before continuing down the trail. Hug-a-Bug stood and waited for us to catch up to her, and once we did, we chased after Branson as far as we could! We continued along and came to a trail junction with the Tonto Trail called the "Tipoff." There was a compost toilet and an emergency phone. We still hadn't caught up with Branson. There were other hikers further down the trail but I couldn't tell if any of them was Branson.

"Well so much for our plan to get close to Branson and try to use time travel to confirm if he has the magical lens," Blaze sighed.

"What should we do? We can't ditch the Adventure Club," Song said.

"I think we should wait here until the rest of the group

catches up to us and then decide what to do. Maybe Papa Lewis will have an idea," I suggested.

It seemed like forever until Papa Lewis, Dad, T2, Tony, Harper and the other kids in the Adventure Club caught up to us.

"Why did you guys take off like that?" Tony asked.

"I'm sorry. I was just being silly. I planned to stop and wait for you guys, but then half the group chased after me, so I just kept going," Hug-a-Bug explained.

"Where's Branson?" Harper asked, looking up ahead for him.

"He kept going. We couldn't catch up to him," I told her.

"Well, we need to get him back with our group. We need to account for everyone, and we can't have kids running off like this. People die out here from the heat and the elements; this is no place to play games," Tony said in a serious tone.

While Tony was talking, I pulled Papa Lewis aside and whispered the situation to him. He thought for a moment, then gave his answer loudly so all of us could hear.

"I think we should split into two groups and meet up at the campground. I can lead the first group down to try and catch up with Branson and anyone that wants to hike at a regular pace can stay back with the second group," Papa Lewis suggested.

"That's a good idea, Lewis. But what if Branson turned onto the Tonto Trail at this junction? Hikers get lost all the time by simply taking a wrong turn at trail junctions like this," Tony reasoned.

"You're absolutely right Tony. We need to be sure he didn't turn onto the wrong trail," Papa Lewis agreed.

While we all stood at the Tipoff discussing our options, three hikers approached us from the west along the Tonto Trail. They all wore evergreen ball caps and gray t-shirts with National Park Service logos on them, which made it obvious that they were NPS employees! Tall poles protruded from their backpacks and towered several feet high over them. They stopped and took their packs off. T2 walked up to them and we all followed him.

"Hello! Did you happen to see a lone hiker pass by in the past 30 minutes?" T2 asked.

"Nope, we haven't seen anybody all morning until now," one of the park service hikers answered. "Why? Are you missing someone?"

"Yeah. A teenager from our group took off down the trail ahead of us and we want to be sure he didn't take a wrong turn onto the Tonto Trail before we continue on down to Bright Angel Campsite for the night," Tony clarified.

The NPS hiker sighed with relief. "Well, today's your lucky day. We're with the National Park Service and this is our rendezvous point for the rest of our group. We have three more from our team walking towards us from the east on the Tonto Trail. If you wait here with us for a little bit, they will be able to verify if your missing hiker took a wrong turn onto the Tonto Trail. We also have radio contact with the National Park Service if we need to call in a search team."

"Wow, that's very gracious of you, thank you," Tony responded.

"What are those huge poles for that are sticking out of your backpacks?" I asked.

"We're park biologists and we're studying the bats. Several times a year, we use these poles to set up nets to catch the bats and check them for white-nose syndrome," one of the other NPS hikers explained.

Hug-a-Bug crinkled her nose "What's white-nose syndrome? Is it what it sounds like?"

"It's a fungus that is actively killing off bats all over the world. We have 22 different species of bats here in Grand Canyon. We catch and release them with these harmless nets to check to see if any of them have it. You can tell if they have white-nose syndrome by a white fungus that forms on their wings," the biologist explained.

"That's a huge number of bat species! I didn't realize there are so many different types of bats in one place! Bats are so creepy. Why go through all of that for a bat?" Hug-a-Bug asked.

Another of the biologists smiled. "Bats are very good for the environment. They eat tons of mosquitos, and they spread seeds of plants which helps with pollination."

"Wow, I had no idea they did all that! You just turned me into a fan of bats," Hug-a-Bug said with a laugh.

Papa Lewis, T2, Dad, Blaze, Song, Hug-a-Bug, and I left Harper, Tony, and the others in the Adventure Club at the Tipoff junction with the Tonto Trail. We continued down the South Kaibab Trail in hopes of catching up with Branson. The trail began to drop dramatically down towards the river. We were now among the oldest rocks in Grand Canyon. We stopped to enjoy an amazing view of the inner gorge and then we began a downward series of switchbacks. There was still no sign of Branson anywhere.

The trail continued to zig-zag down and led us toward a tunnel blasted clean through the rock. Blaze was in the lead and he disappeared into the tunnel with everyone else following behind. Except all of a sudden, he started marching backward, forcing all of us to retreat. He had been face-to-face with the head of the first of a series of mules!

It was so dark in the tunnel that none of us saw the mules coming through and Blaze had saved us from being trampled. We all stepped off the trail and out of the way. A cowboy in the saddle of the lead mule led his team of rider-less mules behind him. Each mule had large empty leather bags strapped to it.

"Coming through! Thanks for stepping out of our way," the cowboy said, tipping his hat. "We just dropped off food supplies and picked up the mail from Phantom Ranch."

After the mule train passed by, we entered the tunnel and popped out the other side onto the Kaibab Suspension Bridge across the murky Colorado River. This bridge was built in 1928 and was still as sturdy as ever. Several rafts were beached below us along the Colorado River just a short walk from where I stood on the bridge.

We passed over the bridge and left the South Kaibab Trail behind us, beginning our hike along the North Kaibab Trail. Something caught my eye on a nearby rock, so I stopped and looked closer. A small lizard had frozen in place and it blended in so well with the reddish rock color that it was almost invisible! I snapped a picture. We followed the trail along the river and soon came across some ruins.

T2 gazed at the remnants. "These are Ancestral Puebloan ruins. They are found throughout Grand Canyon and are fascinating to explore, but we should get to the campground quickly and see if Branson is there. We can come back and check the ruins out later!"

We continued hiking. It sure was much hotter down here at the bottom of Grand Canyon than up on the rim. On the rim, I wore my jacket at times, but ever since we began our hike below the rim, I'd only worn a t-shirt and I just drank my last sip of water.

An inviting rustic log cabin sat off to our left and soon we saw a sign near it that read 'Welcome to Bright Angel Campground.' The campground was spread along a trail paralleling Bright Angel Creek. The campsites were interspersed beneath cottonwood trees that provided much-needed shade from the intense midday sun, and some of the sites had their own covered shelters. I was excited that we were going to camp wedged between some of the oldest rocks in the world, down in a gorge, over a mile deep. We walked until we found the group campsite we were assigned to. It was larger than all the other campsites and it had a covered shelter with stone walls and several picnic tables, plus it was within feet of the creek. Several large metal rectangular cans, similar to military ammunition cans, were anchored to the picnic table benches to secure our food and scented toiletries from animals. It would probably be a while until Tony, Harper, and the others catch up with us. We all sat down to rest, but it was hard to keep calm wondering what happened to Branson.

"Hey, can we complete the Phantom Ranch Junior Ranger program?" Hug-a-Bug suggested. "It's the holy grail of junior ranger programs because you have to come down here to the bottom of Grand Canyon to complete it."

Hug-a-Bug took it upon herself to complete a junior ranger program in every national park that we explore, and Grand Canyon offers three different junior ranger programs: one for the South Rim, one for the North Rim, and one right here at Phantom Ranch. There was no sign of Branson, and we likely had plenty of time before everyone else would arrive.

"That's a splendid idea Hug-a-Bug," Dad answered. "We have some time. Let's walk up to Phantom Ranch to look into the program and check to see if your grandma, your mom, and Sydney made it down here yet."

T2 offered to remain at the camp to watch out for the rest of the group, and with that settled we walked through the campground towards Phantom Ranch.

Little did we know, our luck was about to change.

CHAPTER 13

STUCK IN TIME

We walked past numerous campsites. Some of them had unusual metal poles that campers hung backpacks and other gear from to keep their stuff high up off the ground.

"Those sure are some strange poles in the campsites," I commented.

"Those are the telephone poles installed by the Civilian Conservation Corps, or the CCC," Papa Lewis replied. "You're now standing where CCC's Company 818 used to be. A few hundred CCC workers called this place home for a while."

If you've followed us on other national park adventures, then you know about the CCC that President Franklin Roosevelt created to put our country back to work during the Great Depression. The CCC camps were set up in national parks, national forests, and other places across the United States. They employed young men and paid them 30 dollars a month for their work. They could keep five dollars from each monthly paycheck for personal expenses, but they had to mail the rest home to support their families. CCC workers did hard work. They were supervised by the U.S. Army in camp, but when they went to work, they were supervised by the National Park Service.

"Follow me," Papa Lewis said as he led us away from the other campers and out of sight. "Say, Bubba Jones, could you take us back to 1934?"

I placed my hand on my magic journal and did as Papa Lewis instructed. The sky went dark, a gust of wind pushed against me, and then it was light again. Our clothes had transformed. Us guys wore cotton pants, shirts with suspenders, knee-high boots, and wide-brimmed hats. Hug-a-Bug and Song wore ankle-length dresses and leather boots.

Rows of tents lined two sides of a gravel parade ground. Young CCC men wearing green World-War-I era fatigues and combat boots were everywhere. Two CCC men pulled a reel of telephone wire down the trail. They stopped and fed the phone line up to a man perched on a telephone pole. The man on the pole wrapped the wire around one of the points at the top. He looked down and noticed us watching him work.

"When this is done, you'll be able to make a telephone call from Phantom Ranch," he explained, giving us a wave. "You'll even be able to receive calls out here."

"Wow, that's amazing!" I said, trying to act impressed despite the fact that I was from a future with high-speed internet, cell phones, social media, texting, and GPS satellites.

"Keep up the good work!" Papa Lewis called up to the man, giving him a thumbs-up.

"Will do, sir!" the CCC worker responded.

Papa Lewis led us out of sight after that, and then I huddled us all together and said, "Take us back to the present."

A gust of wind blew, everything went dark again, and then it was light. Our clothes had transformed back into our modern-day hiking clothes. The CCC boys and their camp were gone. Campers milled about. Some set up tents, some sat at picnic tables, and others splashed in the stream. A lonely backpack hung on the same telephone pole that we just watched the CCC men wire up in 1934. The telephone wire was gone and the pole had taken on a new purpose.

"The CCC worked on many projects in Grand Canyon," Papa Lewis noted. "One of their biggest achievements was the trans-canyon phone line. They connected the North Rim and the South Rim by phone line along the South Kaibab Trail, the North Kaibab

Trail, and Phantom Ranch. This telephone line was the best way to communicate with the people of Phantom Ranch until modern technology replaced it in 1982," Papa Lewis explained.

"That CCC worker sure was excited about the phone service," Hug-a-Bug observed.

"You would be, too, if your only communication before the phone was by mule mail down here," Papa Lewis countered, and there wasn't much she could say to that!

We continued our walk over a little bridge to the other side of Bright Angel Creek and turned left onto the North Kaibab Trail. Soon, we passed by a path that led to a park ranger outpost. A short stroll from there brought us to a circular dirt area with large posts, made of river stone, all along the outer perimeter spaced several feet apart. A thick chain ran from post to post, attached to each one, and it looked like it was some kind of arrival and departure corral for the mules. We walked under a sign that hung below a metal bar; it read "Phantom Ranch Welcomes You."

A sprawling compound of small cabins built from river stone and wood gradually became visible. The cabins were scattered throughout the grass-covered landscape, connected by worn dirt paths and shaded by Cottonwood trees. They blended right into the nature surrounding them. This felt like a truly relaxing getaway.

"Guess who designed Phantom Ranch?" Papa Lewis asked as we strolled through the compound.

"It has to be the work of Mary Colter. She blends her building designs in with their surroundings," Hug-a-Bug immediately answered.

"That's right, Hug-a-Bug, Ms. Colter designed these buildings. This particular resort was completed in 1922. Everything is pretty much the way it was then except for the addition of some modern amenities. This was considered a luxurious getaway and some notable celebrities vacationed here long before Grand Canyon's popularity grew. The Canteen is the gathering place for meals and social fun," Papa Lewis explained as we approached a large building similar in design to the cabins.

Hikers lounged about on a bench along the front of the building and in the grass beneath the shade of a nearby Cottonwood tree. We stepped into the Canteen and were welcomed with a blast of ice cold air thanks to the air conditioner. It was a pleasant shock to my system after walking all morning under the hot desert sun! A staff member peered out from behind a counter stocked with bins of snacks, candy, lip balm, sunscreen, other amenities, and souvenirs.

"Welcome! How about a fresh ice-cold lemonade for each of you?" the staff member offered.

We all eagerly accepted, and seconds later I slurped down the most refreshing glass of lemonade I've ever had. Natural daylight from the window-lined walls added to the Canteen's rustic and cheery character. Vaulted ceilings and boardroom-sized tables with log chairs offered plenty of room for guests to sit and eat together. Several people sat reading books, writing postcards, and playing cards. Papa Lewis asked a staff member if Grandma, Mom, and Sydney had arrived yet. The staff member confirmed that they had a room reservation, but they hadn't checked in. Their mule train took the Bright Angel Trail down, which was the path we would hike out tomorrow. Hug-a-Bug and Song found some Phantom Ranch Junior Ranger booklets up near the counter and began reading through the requirements. A leather saddle bag hung on the back wall next to a chalkboard. The saddlebag had a slot in the top and there were some words stamped into the leather: U.S. Mail, Carried by Mule, Phantom Ranch, Arizona.

"That's so cool! You can send postcards by mule from the bottom of Grand Canyon!" I exclaimed.

Dad purchased several postcards and stamps and handed them out to all of us. I slipped mine into my cargo pocket for later so I'd have some time to think about who I could send it to. We stepped back outside into the desert heat and something suddenly caught my eye.

An unwatched backpack that looked just like Branson's sat on the bench beside the Canteen door. I hadn't notice it before when we'd walked into the Canteen because it was blocked from view with all the hikers that were there. A pamphlet was folded open and wedged partially underneath the backpack, so I picked it up to get a closer look. The pamphlet was a National Park historical walking tour guide, titled "Phantoms of the Past." A 'Mailed by Mule' postcard with Branson's return address written on it was also tucked underneath the pack.

Branson is here, I realized. I looked all around for him, but he was nowhere in sight, so I ran back inside the Canteen. Still, no Branson. I looked back at the pamphlet, trying to find any clue I could. It was open to page five and someone had drawn a circle around the fourth stop of the historical guide: "Swimming Pool." The circle was drawn with the same color pen that was used on Branson's postcard. I'd read about the canyon's highlighted swimming pool before. In 1934, the CCC dug out a rock-lined swimming pool here at Phantom Ranch. It even had its own little waterfall! But in 1972, the pool was filled in and it no longer exists. I knew exactly what Branson was up to. *He went for a swim!*

"Hey guys!" I called to the others. "Come here, I think I know where Branson went!"

Papa Lewis, Hug-a-Bug, Blaze, and Song huddled around me. I showed them Branson's gear and the pamphlet.

"He must've gone back in time to take a swim. How about we join him? Follow me!" I said as I slipped Branson's postcard and pamphlet into my pocket. Song, Blaze, and Hug-a-Bug cheered in approval.

I led everyone to the area described in the pamphlet between cabins five and six. There was a slight dip in the terrain there that was covered with weeds, and it seemed to be a perfect fit for the pool's description. We huddled together near the edge, and I said, "Take us back to 1934."

The sky went dark. A gust of wind pushed against me, and then it was light again. All of us wore bathing suits.

A dozen people swam in what was now a glittering pool right next to us.

"Come on in, the water's great!" one of them shouted to us.

We looked at each other, shrugged, and jumped right in! As soon as I hit the water, I felt a jolt of bitter cold. Wow! Even though it was blazing hot outside the water still managed to be freezing, honestly a great way to stay cool prior to the invention of air conditioning. I climbed up onto a rock on the edge of the in-ground pool and scanned the area. Branson was nowhere in sight. Everyone searched the compound everywhere for him, but it seemed my hunch was incorrect. After we all finished our searching, we huddled together in another secluded place nearby. I said, "Take us back to the present."

The sky went dark, a gust of wind blew, and then it was light again. We were back in the present standing alongside all that remained of the pool: a slight depression in the ground.

"I don't get it. Where could he be?" I said, frustrated.

Blaze met my eyes, his gaze sympathetic. "I don't know," he answered, "but that was amazing. To go back in time and take a cool dip in a pool that doesn't exist anymore? We didn't find Branson, but that was still awesome."

We all sat down together at a nearby picnic table. I pulled the pamphlet out of my pocket and tossed it in the middle. I thought I had figured out what happened to Branson, but I was wrong. Now what? If we couldn't locate him, we'd need to report him missing and a massive search-and-rescue operation would ensue! I sat in silence, thinking through our situation. Hug-a-Bug picked up the booklet and flipped through it.

"Hey Bubba Jones, look, there's another place in here that's circled," she said, pointing to another page. "It's the first stop on the historic tour, Rust's Camp. We might as well try there!"

Hug-a-Bug's discovery instilled some hope in us that perhaps we'd find Branson yet. We followed her along the trail, out of the camp, past the ranger station, and up to a corral with several mules. The mules rested under the corral's roof and some trees; they'd probably just finished hauling supplies and people down from the rim.

"This is where Rust's Camp used to be. In 1907, before Phantom Ranch was built, David Rust established a remote camp here with tents. His camp became a destination for hunters and tourists. He installed a cable tramway to help people safely and easily get across the Colorado River," Hug-a-Bug explained as she skimmed the "Phantoms of the Past" booklet.

We huddled together again, and I looked at everyone in turn and said, "Take us back to 1907."

Everything went dark, a gust of wind blew, and then it was light again. I opened my eyes and looked around. Our clothes were similar to what we wore when we'd met Mary Colter. The mules and the corral were gone and in their place were several large canvas tents assembled over wooden decks. Several picnic tables and fire pits were scattered between the tents and the area was almost fully shaded with freshly planted Cottonwoods.

We were all eager to check out the tram as we scanned the area for any sign of Branson. We walked down to the river's edge. A cable was stretched across the river about 60 feet up in the air. Off in the distance, a man who fit the description of David Rust stood on a rock next to a wooden pully system, where the cable was anchored to the shore. The man turned a hand crank winch and a small caged platform that dangled above the river inched towards the riverbank, swinging back and forth in the occasional strong canyon wind. The two passengers in the tram looked terrified as it slowly edged closer to shore. If the cable were to snap, they would fall to their certain deaths in the fast-moving current of the Colorado River.

"No way! That's not for me! I wouldn't trust that thing with my life," Hug-a-Bug insisted.

Blaze nodded quickly. "Mhm, yep, agreed. I don't want to ride on that."

"I think the thrill of riding that rickety thing across the river was part of the adventure of visiting Rust's Camp!" Papa Lewis offered. He took in our skeptical faces, and decided to change the subject. "We don't need to ride it. Let's focus on finding Branson."

"Hey, how did you guys get here?" a familiar voice shouted.

I pivoted toward the voice, and there he was! Branson!

"Better question: how did you get here?" I countered, relieved. We'd finally found him.

I thought he'd be excited or proud having somehow found a way to use the time travel lens, but he actually looked frightened. "I'm stuck here," he said, his voice wavering. "I can't figure out how to go back to the present." He hesitated, glancing at Blaze before looking straight down at his feet. "I confess, Blaze, I found your lens, and I took it. When I experienced that super realistic vision of the ancient lake yesterday while we were looking for Hug-a-Bug and Bubba Jones, I knew it had to be because of something magic. What else could it be? And when I saw Blaze freak out and hide the lens, I knew it *had* to be special somehow. I love history and geology and...." Branson trailed off. He looked more and more embarrassed with every word he said.

"Don't worry, Branson," Song said, her voice kind. "We're here to help. But we need to know what happened."

Branson shook his head. "I love geology," he began again. "And my dad suggested that I join this program that matches students up to research our national parks. My dad requested that the organization pair me with Arthur from Acadia National Park. I didn't know why he did that at first. But then he told me that his friend witnessed a family disappear and reappear in Acadia National Park and overheard them talking about traveling through time. My dad fantasized about time travel magic, how if it really was real, then we could use it to explore, and look for ancient treasure, and potentially even get rich.

"My dad convinced his friend to hire a private

investigator to dig up anything he could about this family. He discovered that their son, Arthur, was part of this National Park project. He hoped that if I was paired up with Arthur, I might be able to learn more about how the time travel magic works. The investigator also discovered that some other potential time traveler, relatives of Arthur's, reside here in the Grand Canyon, and they have a rapid reaction team that travels from park to park to help solve mysteries, but he couldn't dig up anything else on them.

"Arthur never revealed any time travel secrets to me, which really disappointed my dad, but I got lucky when I recognized the effects of the magical lens, and saw Blaze hiding it! I knew my dad would be proud of me for finding it." He sighed. "It sounds stupid now, but that's why I took the lens, and I hid it, and I lied. I put it in a telescope my dad got for me, and just switched out the lenses. My dad was going to meet up with the Adventure Club at Phantom Ranch; he took a mule there this morning, and I planned on running ahead of the group to meet him and get our own special time travel adventure in before you all caught up. I met up with him, and we successfully time traveled here, and my dad thought it was super cool! We were having a lot of fun, the most fun ever, actually. But I let him take the telescope 'cause he wanted to try using it to take us back, and then he just vanished right before my eyes, just like that, and I haven't seen him since."

"How close were you to your dad when he vanished?" I asked.

"I was down here by the river and he was up over there, about twenty feet away," Branson answered.

I didn't want to share any of our time travel secrets with Branson, but I knew that would be too far away for him and his father to time travel together.

"Where is the telescope now?"

"My dad had it in his hand when he vanished," Branson answered.

"Do you know where your dad planned to go with the telescope?"

"No! But before this happened, we figured that someone might try and track us down to get the lens back, so we had to be sneaky. If we got separated, we planned to send each other a postcard with a time and place to meet back up. That's difficult to do though if you're stuck back in time. I have a postcard, but it's with my backpack on the bench in front of the Canteen back in the present. If you get me back to the present time, I can send my dad a postcard to link back up with him."

So far, his story checked out with everything we had found.

"Branson, I'm Lewis, Bubba Jones's grandfather," Papa Lewis introduced himself, placing a hand on his shoulder. "Wait here for a minute while we have a private conversation, okay? We'll figure out a way to get you back to the present."

"O-okay, sir," Branson said, his voice tinged with fear.

We huddled together to make a plan far enough away so Branson couldn't overhear us. Even though we'd found him, we still needed to get the lens back. We decided that our best strategy was to meet up with Branson's dad and secure the telescope.

As we walked back over to Branson, I noticed he looked almost as if he was about to cry. "I don't want to be stuck here forever," he said.

I extended a hand for him to take. "Don't worry," I replied. "You won't be."

CHAPTER 14

STARS & SCORPIONS

"**W**e can get you back to the present, but we need you to help us get the lens back from your dad," I explained.

Branson nodded. "Okay, yeah, that's fine. I mean, I got to go back in time with him once. That's enough for me."

I pulled out his postcard from my pocket and explained to him that we found his backpack and the historic tour pamphlet that allowed us to track him to Rust's Camp. I instructed him to write the following on the postcard: "Meet me on the top floor of the Desert

View Watchtower on Thursday at 1 pm."

Branson did as I asked. Song had suggested the Desert View Watchtower as the meetup location; it was another Mary Colter creation. After Branson finished penning the note, I took his postcard. My dad and I left everyone at Rust's Camp, found a hidden spot out of the way, and together we time traveled back to the present. I pulled Branson's postcard out of my cargo pocket and I made a little edit to his note, squeezing a "2" in between "1" and "pm." This way, if Branson tried to keep the time travel lens and deceive us, we would be there with his dad an hour early and able to stop him.

I entered the Canteen and dropped the postcard into the "Mailed by Mule" postcard pouch. I'd picked the perfect moment to do this, 'cause almost immediately a staff member took the mail pouch, opened it up, and dumped it into a U.S. Post Office bin. She handed it to a man who was tasked with bringing the mail up from Phantom Ranch with his mule team. The man explained that since this was going to an address here in the park, it would arrive at the address on Wednesday, the day before our rendezvous at Desert View Watchtower. He also said this was the last mail pick up for today and walked out the door of the Canteen. If Branson tried to send another postcard, it wouldn't arrive until after our Dessert View Watchtower meetup.

Dad and I walked back to the mule corral and time traveled back to Rust's Camp. We linked back up with Papa Lewis, Hug-a-Bug, Blaze, Song, and Branson. I explained that I successfully mailed the postcard. But before we brought Branson back to the present, I wanted to find the answer to one more unsolved mystery.

"Hey Branson, why did you ask if the past could be altered so that Grand Canyon didn't exist?"

"How did you know I said that?" Branson shot back, but then he took a deep breath to calm himself down. "I would never do anything to harm Grand Canyon. I just wondered if this magic could be used to alter the past. I've never been exposed to time travel magic and I wanted to know how powerful it was."

I sighed. "That's fair. Just so you know, all of us here, we're all from the same family and we've been entrusted to protect our time travel magic at all costs from falling into the wrong hands. We were given the gift of time travel in order to learn from the past so we can protect our wildlands for future generations. The magic can't change anything about the past; it can just bring us there and back. Listen, Branson, no one else in the adventure group knows about our time travel abilities, and we need to keep it that way."

Branson nodded, and he looked more sincere than I'd ever seen him before. "Don't worry, I won't say anything," he murmured. "I just want to go back to the present and forget all of this happened."

We all huddled into a circle. I held my time travel journal behind my back so that Branson couldn't see it. The less he knew about our family secret, the better. I then said, "Take us back to the present!"

Everything went dark, a gust of wind blew, and then it was light again. We all wore our modern clothes and we were standing alongside the mule corral. We walked up the trail to the Canteen, Branson secured his backpack, and then we headed back to our group's campsite.

Tony, Harper, and the rest of the Adventure Club had arrived. Everyone was excited that we'd found Branson and he didn't say a word about what had happened; he kept our secret safe. Tony and Harper pulled Branson aside and scolded him for running off down the trail alone, and I'm not sure what Branson said to them, but I'm sure he was apologetic. Papa Lewis, Dad, and T2 walked over to set up their own tent nearby and they quietly updated T2 on the situation at hand.

Tony and Harper reviewed the camping rules with our group. Papa Lewis, T2, Dad, Blaze, Song, Hug-a-Bug, and I wandered back up to Phantom Ranch and saw Mom, Sydney, and Grandma Lewis dismounting from their mules; they had just arrived! We helped them get settled into their room and then us kids walked down to the Ranger Station so Song and Hug-a-Bug could turn in their Junior Ranger booklets. A backcountry ranger asked them both a few questions and then they raised their right hands and took the Junior Ranger Pledge. The ranger signed their booklets and time-stamped them, and that was that. They'd done it!

We walked back up to our campsite for dinner. We'd packed two stoves and enough freeze-dried meals for all of us. These meals just required boiling water; once that was mixed in, they were ready to eat. We were given a choice between chicken teriyaki, chili mac, and lasagna. After dinner, everyone helped clean our utensils and secure our trash, food, and toiletries back in the metal cans.

As soon as the sun set, the air became instantly cooler, cool enough for a jacket even. Our campground grew dark as the night sky lit up with stars. Our entire group walked up to the amphitheater for the evening ranger talk. It was an interesting presentation, a historical overview of Phantom Ranch. One child in the audience asked about snakes, and the ranger explained that there are several types of snakes in Grand Canyon, including the venomous Grand Canyon rattlesnake, which is pink in color.

The ranger reviewed some of the other wildlife in the area with us, too. He talked about some of the desert scrub plants, and he ended his talk with some facts about the bark scorpion. They're arachnids, so they're related to spiders, and they're about three inches long and resemble a lobster, only way smaller. The tip of the bark scorpian's tail has a stinger that releases a neurotoxin, and they will only sting you if they feel threatened. But the sting can cause some health concerns, so you should get medical treatment immediately if you're stung. They're hard to see and they're nocturnal.

The ranger pulled out a blacklight and at the end of the program we followed him along the trail. He explained that the bark scorpion is fluorescent and shows up in blacklight. He shone his light onto the trail and sure enough, we saw several scorpions!

The night sky was amazing. The shadows cast by the Canyon walls and the absence of manmade light made the stars in the sky appear brighter than ever. I could see way more stars than I normally see when I look up at the sky at night. It was so stunning that I sat and enjoyed the view until my eyes grew too tired to stay open. I zipped into my tent and fell asleep almost instantly.

CHAPTER 15

THUMBS UP!

In the morning, I unzipped my tent door and stepped out into the fresh air. Soon everyone was up and preparing to hike. We prepared freeze-dried bacon and eggs for breakfast, which was delicious. Papa Lewis, T2, Dad, Tony, and Harper sipped on coffee. As soon as the sun broke into the canyon, it would get hot and we had a hard, long hike ahead of us. The hike down along the South Kaibab Trail yesterday was the easier leg. We planned to take the Bright Angel Trail back up to the South Rim. The Bright Angel Trail is longer than the South Kaibab Trail, but it has water along it and the incline wouldn't be as dramatic. Even so, it is recommended to allow yourself twice as much time to scale the canyon as you do to hike down it.

Before we departed, T2, Dad, Blaze, Song, Hug-a-Bug and I slipped out of camp and walked over to Phantom Ranch to update Mom, Sydney, and Grandma Lewis on the mission. We let them know that we hoped to have the time travel lens back by tomorrow (Thursday) and we filled them in on what had transpired so far. The three of them had enjoyed a steak dinner last night and they'd just finished a yummy breakfast. Their mule team planned to head right up the trail we'd hiked down yesterday, so we wouldn't see them until the conclusion of our hike at Bright Angel Lodge. We all hugged goodbye and headed back to our campsite to break camp.

We packed everything up, including our trash, put on our backpacks, and walked quietly out of camp so we wouldn't disturb sleeping campers. We backtracked to the ancient ruins that we had passed on our arrival yesterday. Just off the trail, there were some rock wall foundation remnants that I was sure had a story behind them.

"Song and Blaze asked us if they could put together a presentation about the first humans here in Grand Canyon and share it with you all," Harper said, motioning for Blaze and Song to come up and stand in front of everyone. Hug-a-Bug and I looked at each other; we didn't know they were going to present like Branson did!

Song spoke first. "The first humans to inhabit Grand Canyon can be traced as far back as 12,000 years ago, after the Ice Age. They're known as Paleo Indians. One of their Clovis points, which are tools with projectile points used for hunting, was found in the Grand Canyon area."

"These ruins here are Puebloan and date back a few thousand years," Blaze continued, motioning to the structures around him. "30 to 40 Puebloan families once called this place home from A.D. 1050 to A.D 1140. Ruins like these are scattered throughout Grand Canyon. Less than ten percent of the Park has been explored for artifacts and fossils. The larger ruin of a building that is shaped differently was the kiva, a room used for ceremonies and meetings."

"Puebloans ate cacti, agave, and other vegetation easily found here. They farmed corn, made baskets, and hunted bighorn sheep and deer. There are thousands of caves throughout Grand Canyon and split-twig figurines have been discovered in many of these caves," added Song. "These figurines are typically made from a single stick to resemble the shape of a deer or a bighorn sheep. There are also ancient etchings known as petroglyphs and paintings on rocks known as pictographs of people and animals."

"Eleven active native tribes are historically tied to Grand Canyon. The Hopi are descendants of the Puebloans and are considered one of the oldest cultures in the world. The Hopi refer to Grand Canyon as 'Ongtupqa,' which means 'salt canyon' in English. The Havasupai have been in the Grand Canyon region for 800 years. They are the only tribe that lives in the bottom of Grand Canyon, in Supai, a village only accessible by foot. 'Havasupai' means 'People of the Blue-Green Waters.' Their reservation is home to the beautiful

Havasupai Falls. The Hualapai, which means 'People of the Tall Pines,' built a circular skywalk tourist attraction with a glass floor that extends out into the canyon." Blaze paused and looked at Song before continuing. "We're Navajo, like our father and our aunt. The Navajo are the largest of Grand Canyon's eleven active tribes. All of the tribes here suffered through European colonization and settlement. Many tribes' ancestral lands were taken from them." Blaze sighed, shaking his head. "Some of their territories have been given back, but not all of them."

"We're still here," Song concluded. "Grand Canyon is our home and our history, and that won't be forgotten."

We all clapped for Song and Blaze, then Tony and Harper thanked them for their presentation. Together we all left the Puebloan ruins and followed signs to the Bright Angel Trail to begin our hike back up to the rim. The trail led us along the edge of the Colorado River and onto the Silver Bridge.

CHAPTER 16

ABOUT THAT TELESCOPE

I wondered if we would ever run into Wild Bill. He said he would check in on how things were going down here, but no one had seen him yet. We even worked out a simple code signal if we saw him. If everything was going okay and we didn't need his help, we'd give him a thumbs-up sign, but if we needed his assistance, we would give him a thumbs-down sign. He went off the grid on his own adventure in the park, and no one had heard from him in a few days.

I stopped halfway across the bridge, perched at least 30 feet above the river, mesmerized by the morning view as I looked upstream. The sun had not yet risen high enough up into the sky to cook us down here in the desert. Its light sparkled in the rapids. My trance-like gaze was interrupted by a lone raft floating beneath me as it headed downriver. A man in the raft waved enthusiastically at me. I waved back and then realized it was Wild Bill! And he wasn't alone; as he steered the raft, a woman sat content next to him. She clutched her paddle and had a wide smile across her face.

"This is Rosemary!" Wild Bill introduced as his raft continued downriver beneath us.

We all waved back and then Papa Lewis, Dad, Hug-a-Bug and I gave him our secret code 'thumbs-up,' signaling that we did not need his help right now. He gave us a thumbs up back and his raft grew smaller and smaller until it disappeared downriver.

We slowly snaked our way up out of the Inner Gorge. The rocks were clearly different in texture and color here than the rock layers higher up. The trail followed the Colorado River downstream and then turned upward away from the river. We all noticed a cave not far from the trail.

The ranger program last night made me more aware of some of the desert plants. I was excited when I spotted a Utah agave, a twelve-foot-tall yellow flowering stalk that reached up towards the sky from jagged green leaves near the ground. The Utah agave flowers only once between 15 and 25 years of age, and then it dies. I could also identify some of the desert scrub by name as I hiked along, like the prickly pear cactus, the hedgehog cactus and the banana yucca.

We climbed up through a series of switchbacks known as the Devil's Corkscrew. Blaze and Song noticed some neat pictographs on nearby rocks. We stopped for a long break at Indian Garden, a trailside campground with a ranger station. Everyone took advantage of the water tap and topped off their water.

Branson had remained quiet for the entire hike up. After our long break, we continued our trek upward. I noticed the temperature had cooled down. It was colder than the morning temperature at the bottom. We passed by the Three Mile and the Mile-and-a-Half Rest-houses. But we had plenty of water, so we didn't stop. Soon, we began to run into lots of people walking down from the rim without any gear or supplies which signaled to us that we were near the top!

Moments later, I could hear vehicles and lots of voices. We'd made it up to the rim! We walked past Kolb Studio, then Lookout Studio, and then finally Bright Angel Lodge. We did it!

Tony and Harper led us over to the ice-cream parlor behind the lodge. They congratulated us on our accomplishment and said that we'd all earned ourselves some ice-cream. Yum!

Most of the Adventure Club would depart this afternoon on the train back to Williams, everyone except for Branson, Blaze, Song, Hug-a-Bug and me. We all planned to spend one last night at the lodge, as we still had some business to attend to. Since we had a smaller group, we all stayed together in Buckey's cabin. This was a relief for me, 'cause it made it easy to keep a close eye on Branson. The girls took one room and the boys took the other.

Despite our big hike today, everyone was too anxious about the missing lens to sleep. Morning took forever to arrive. A knock at the door at eight in the morning startled me from my bed. Someone had slid a note underneath the door. I opened it, and it read "Branson, change of plans, meet me today at Hopi Point instead of Dessert Watchtower, same time. Love, Dad."

Seemed like Branson's dad thought his son still had this room all to himself. I read the note out loud to everyone.

"My dad is probably worried that our meet up point might be compromised. So, he switched the location," Branson explained.

"That's fine. We're coming with you to Hopi Point. That is just a short shuttle bus ride along Hermit Road from here," I assured him.

"That's cool, Bubba Jones. I don't want anything to do with this time travel business anymore. That was the scariest thing ever when I was stuck back in time."

Hug-a-Bug and Song slipped out to go alert Papa Lewis, T2, Dad, Mom, Sydney, and Grandma about the meetup change. I didn't let Branson know that I had changed his meet up time to noon. Our entire crew boarded the red bus towards Hermit's Rest. This was a very scenic route along the South Rim with several views that are considered some of the best of Grand Canyon.

After several stops, the bus pulled over and the driver shouted, "Hopi Point!"

We all exited the bus and walked right up to a stunning view. A man who looked like an adult version of Branson stood looking out at the canyon, and he had a day pack slung over one shoulder. Branson approached his father and we all converged and circled around them.

"I believe that you have something that belongs to me," T2 declared as he looked at Branson's dad.

"Dad, I told them everything," Branson began. "You don't want to mess with this time travel magic. I got stuck in the past! It was horrible! You vanished and I was all alone stuck in 1907. These guys saved me and brought me back. I told them I would make sure they got there lens back from you. Please give it back to them," he explained.

Branson's dad embraced his son in a hug and then he pulled a telescope out of his daypack and handed it to T2. T2 twisted the lens off the end and inspected it carefully. "Yep, this is it. Thank you!" T2 said as he twisted it back onto his own time travel telescope and handed Branson's dad the telescope with a missing lens.

Branson walked over to me and said, "I'm sorry for any harm that I caused. I love geology and history and when I discovered that you really could time travel, I wanted to experience it."

"I forgive you, Branson. I understand. But, as you discovered, time travel can be dangerous. That's why we must keep it a secret and protect it at all costs," I explained as we shook hands. I turned back to everyone and said with a smile, "Mission complete!"

We all high-fived each other and caught the next shuttle bus back to the main visitor center and watched an amazing Grand Canyon video at the visitor center. Then, we rented bikes and Blaze and Song led us along on a thrilling ride with more spectacular views. T2 picked us up in a large van and he drove us out to Desert View Watchtower. Mary Colter made sure it included authentic Hopi art and a kiva. The view of Grand Canyon from the top of the tower was stunning. We went on a ranger-led tour of the Tusayan Ruins and explored the Tusayan museum, too. The interpretive ranger program of the ruins was fascinating, and the museum highlighted the Native American heritage here in Grand Canyon.

Over the next few days, we branched out and visited the Hualapai Reservation and walked out onto their skywalk. We hiked to Havasupai Falls on the Havasupai Reservation. Hug-a-Bug completed the Junior Ranger competencies and was sworn in for a second time as a Junior Ranger in Grand Canyon.

One thing I learned from our time here is that Grand Canyon is grand for many reasons. There were so many places in the park that we had not yet seen, like the North Rim, which was still encased in snow. One thing was for sure, I wanted to come back again. Grand Canyon truly is an amazing place to explore. Each day that we were here, we had one great adventure after another. But there were still many more grand adventures waiting to happen!

The last night in the park, T2 treated us to dinner at the El Tovar Hotel. He thanked us for helping him get his magic telescope lens back. After dinner, we took a casual stroll along the Rim Trail.

"Fred Harvey had strict rules for the women that worked in his hotels and lodges," T2 commented. "Fred Harvey had a dress code and one of the rules of employment was that the women were not allowed to date while they were employed with Fred Harvey. According to folklore, when the CCC men were here in the park, one CCC man really liked one of the Harvey girls but she couldn't have a relationship with him. He wanted to win her heart, so he embedded a heart-shaped stone in this rock wall," T2 explained as he stopped next to the knee-high rock wall that serves as a barrier from the edge of the rim.

Embedded in the wall beneath the top layer of stone was, wouldn't you know it, a heart-shaped stone. Wild Bill and Rosemary happened to be seated on the wall beside it.

"Fancy meeting you here," Wild Bill said as he stood up to greet us. I ran up to give him a hug and he hugged me right back. We all stood there and enjoyed the view as we talked.

Blaze and Song thanked us for helping them get the lens back. I let them know how much we enjoyed exploring Grand Canyon with them. Hug-a-Bug walked over to me and handed me a 'Mailed by Mule' postcard sent from Phantom Ranch. It was addressed to

Hug-a-Bug and me.

"This was in our mailbox at the lodge," she told me, raising an eyebrow.

The note read "Dear Bubba Jones and Hug-a-Bug, we heard about your success in Grand Canyon and we need your help to solve another National Park mystery. We will send coded details shortly."

I handed the postcard to Papa Lewis and he passed it along to our family. Everyone cracked a smile as they read the postcard knowing that already, yet another adventure awaited!

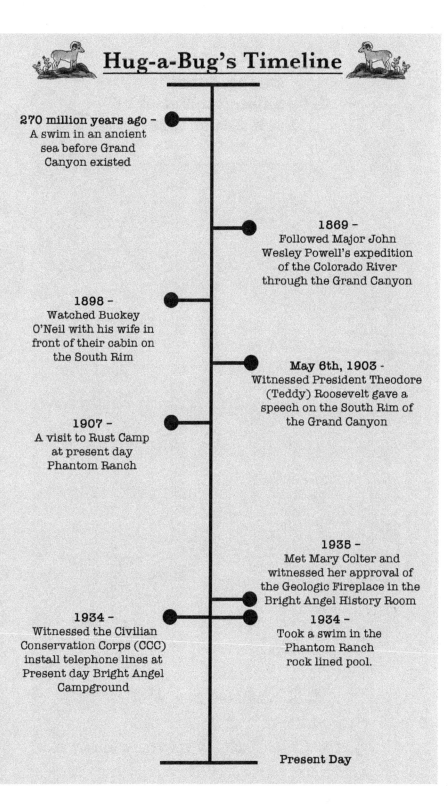

Hug-a-Bug's Timeline

270 million years ago –
A swim in an ancient sea before Grand Canyon existed

1869 –
Followed Major John Wesley Powell's expedition of the Colorado River through the Grand Canyon

1898 –
Watched Buckey O'Neil with his wife in front of their cabin on the South Rim

May 6th, 1903 –
Witnessed President Theodore (Teddy) Roosevelt gave a speech on the South Rim of the Grand Canyon

1907 –
A visit to Rust Camp at present day Phantom Ranch

1935 –
Met Mary Colter and witnessed her approval of the Geologic Fireplace in the Bright Angel History Room

1934 –
Witnessed the Civilian Conservation Corps (CCC) install telephone lines at Present day Bright Angel Campground

1934 –
Took a swim in the Phantom Ranch rock lined pool.

Present Day

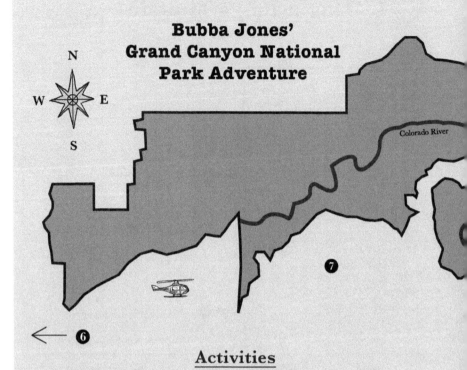

Bubba Jones'
Grand Canyon National
Park Adventure

Colorado River

7

← **6**

Activities

 Helicopter Ride

 Junior Ranger Program

 Raft the Colorado River

 Backpack to Bright Angel Campground

 Locate the Heart Shaped Rock in the wall along the South Rim Trail

 Day Hike

 Bike the South Rim

 Mule Ride

 Train Ride (Williams to Grand Canyon National Park)

👣 Hiking Trips 👣

A South Kaibab Trail   **C** Rim Trail

B Bright Angel Trail   **D** The Trail of Time Walk

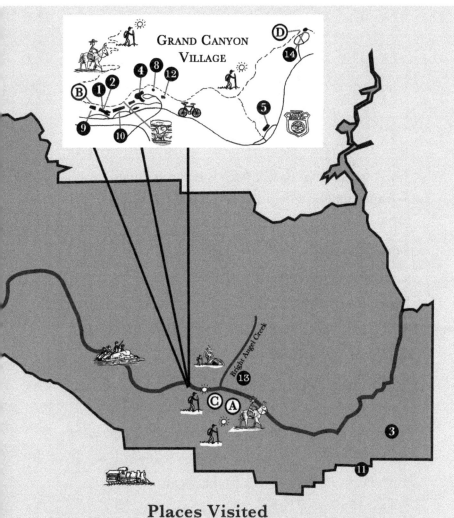

Places Visited

1. Bright Angel Lodge
2. Bright Angel Lodge History Room
3. Desert View Watch Tower
4. El Tovar Hotel
5. Grand Canyon National Park Visitor Center
6. Grand Canyon Skywalk
7. Havasupai Falls
8. Hopi House
9. Kolb Studio
10. Lookout Studio
11. Tusayan Ruins & Museum
12. Verkamp's Visitor Center
13. Phantom Ranch
14. Yavapai Geologic Museum

CURRICULUM GUIDE

The Adventures of Bubba Jones is recommended for grades 3-7 and may be a helpful resource for several curriculum topics.

Social Studies	*Science*
Civilian Conservation Corps	Abert's Squirrel
Hopi Native Americans	Grand Canyon Bats
Ancestral Puebloan People	Desert Bighorn Sheep
Major John Wesley Powell	California Condor
Mary Colter	Elk
National Parks	Grand Canyon Geology
Native Americans who call Grand Canyon home	Grand Canyon Rattlesnake
	Kaibob Squirrel
Theodore Roosevelt	Mule Deer
William "Buckey" O'Neill	Ponderosa Pine
	Ringtail

DISCUSSION QUESTIONS

Chapter 1

1. Who was Major John Wesley Powell?

2. What was Grand Canyon referred to on maps before it was explored?

Chapter 2

1. How many times did Major John Wesley Powell explore the Grand Canyon?

2. How did the Jones family know that the messenger in the helicopter was the right one?

Chapter 3

1. What river formed Grand Canyon?

2. What magic tool is missing?

Chapter 4

1. In the early 1900s, what was the best way to get to Grand Canyon?

2. Which president made Grand Canyon a national monument?

Chapter 5

1. Where in Grand Canyon are the oldest rocks?

2. What was strange about Bubba Jones and Hug-a-Bugs trip to the ancient sea?

Chapter 6

1. Why were Bubba Jones and Hug-a-Bug suspicious of Branson, Blaze and Song?

2. How many years did it take for the Grand Canyon to form?

Chapter 7

1. True or False: The California Condor went extinct.

2. What animal was the park volunteer monitoring?

3. What was significant about Mary Colter?

Chapter 8

1. What is the Hopi House?

Chapter 9

1. How did Blaze and Song learn about the time travel magic?

2. Why are Bubba Jones and Hug a bug suspicious of Branson?

Chapter 10

1. How did Blaze and Song try to see if Branson stole the lens?

2. Who was William "Buckey" O'Neill?

Chapter 11

1. What is one difference between an Abert's squirrel and Kaibab Squirrel?

2. True or False: There are mountain lions in Grand Canyon.

Chapter 12

1. What event makes Bubba Jones even more suspicious of Branson?

2. How many Junior Ranger programs are in the park?

3. What is the name of the ranch at the bottom of the Grand Canyon?

Chapter 13

1. What did the Civilian Conservation Corps (CCC) construct in the bottom of Grand Canyon?

2. What time period was Branson found in?

Chapter 14

1. What lives in Grand Canyon and is florescent?

Chapter 15

1.   How many active Native American tribes are tied to the Grand Canyon?

2.   How were some Native Americans impacted by settlement?

Chapter 16

1.   Who stole the lens?

2.   Do you think they had bad intentions?

BIBLIOGRAPHY

A Living Canyon: Discovering Life at Grand Canyon, Grand Canyon, AZ, National Park Service, U.S. Department of the Interior

About the Hualapai Tribe, accessed July 7, 2019, http://hualapai-nsn.gov/about-2/

Alt, Jeff. *The Adventures of Bubba Jones: Time Traveling Through Acadia National Park*, New York City, NY, Beaufort Books Publishers, 2018

Alt, Jeff. *The Adventures of Bubba Jones: Time Traveling Through Shenandoah National Park*, New York City, NY, Beaufort Books Publishers, 2016

Alt, Jeff. *The Adventures of Bubba Jones: Time Traveling Through the Great Smoky Mountains*, New York City, NY, Beaufort Books Publishers, 2015

Alt, Jeff. *Get Your Kids Hiking: How to Start Them Young and Keep it Fun!*, New York City, NY: Beaufort Books Publishers, 2013

American Indians at Grand Canyon – Past and Present, accessed November 23, 2019, https://grandcanyon.com/planning/american-indians-at-grand-canyon-past-and-present/

Annerino, John, *Hiking the Grand Canyon*, San Francisco, CA, Sierra Club Books, 1986

Best of the Grand Canyon Rafting Trips, accessed July 1, 2019, https://www.riveradventures.com/grand-canyon-rafting/best-of-the-grand-canyon-rafting-trips/

Betz, Eric, *Powell's Grand Ambition – Rafting Through the Grand Canyon*, accessed June 23, 2019, https://www.mygrandcanyonpark.com/park/john-wesley-powell

Bright Angel Lodge, accessed August 12, 2019, https://www.grandcanyonlodges.com/lodging/bright-angel-lodge-cabins/

Brouhard, Rod, How to Treat a Scorpian Sting, November 9, 2019, accessed November 24, 2019, https://www.verywellhealth.com/how-to-treat-a-scorpion-sting-1298271

California Condor, accessed November 25, 2019, https://www.nps.gov/articles/california-condor.htm

California Condor Reintroduction & Recovery, accessed November 17, 2019, https://www.nps.gov/articles/california-condor-recovery.htm

Chin, Jason, *Grand Canyon*, New York, NY, Roaring Brook Press, 2017

Current Bat Research, accessed November 17, 2019, https://www.nps.gov/grca/learn/nature/current-bat-research.htm

Desert Bighorn Sheep, accessed November 13, 2019, https://home.nps.gov/articles/desert-bighorn-sheep.htm

8 Facts About the Grand Canyon You Never Knew, July 26, 2016, accessed July 4, 2019 https://www.nationalparks.org/connect/blog/8-facts-about-grand-canyon-you-never-knew

El Tovar Hotel, accessed August 2, 2019, https://www.grandcanyonlodges.com/lodging/el-tovar-hotel/

Explorers, accessed June 24, 2019, https://www.nps.gov/grca/learn/historyculture/explorers.htm

Fenci, Amanda, *Tribal Relations and Conflicts around the Grand Canyon National Park*, Winter 2015, accessed September 16, 2019, https://watershed.ucdavis.edu/education/classes/files/content/page/Fencl_ECL290_FinalPaper.pdf

Fossils, accessed September 2, 2019, https://www.nps.gov/grca/learn/nature/fossils.htm

Freeman, Melanie Stetson, *How Old is the Grand Canyon? You Might be Surprised*, Christian Science Monitor, January 27, 2014, accessed August 26, 2019, https://www.csmonitor.com/Science/2014/0127/How-old-is-the-Grand-Canyon-You-might-be-surprised

Geology, accessed August 25, 2019, https://www.nps.gov/grca/learn/nature/grca-geology.htm

Geology pt 3: Rock Types in National Parks, accessed August 10, 2019, https://www.nps.gov/teachers/classrooms/geology-pt-3-rock-types-in-national-parks.htm

Glenn Canyon Float Trips, accessed July 5, 2019, https://www.riveradventures.com/glen-canyon-float-trips/glen-canyon-float-trip-experience/full-day/

Grand Canyon Civilian Conservation Corps, accessed November 20, 2019, https://www.nps.gov/grca/learn/historyculture/ccc.htm

Grand Canyon Bright Angel Trail Guide, Grand Canyon National Park, AZ, Grand Canyon Association, 2004

Grand Canyon South Kaibab Trail Guide, Grand Canyon National Park, AZ, Grand Canyon Association, 2006

Grand Canyon Unified School District, accessed August 8, 2019, https://www.grandcanyonschool.org/

Grand Canyon Unified School District, accessed August 8, 2019https://www.publicschoolreview.com/arizona/grand-canyon-unified/403550-school-district/middle

Holden, Courtney, *Grand Canyon's Native American Tribes and Indian Nations*, September, 2018, accessed September 16, 2019, https://www.mygrandcanyonpark.com/park/native-american-tribes

Grattan, Virginia L., *Mary Colter: Builder Upon the Red Earth*, Grand Canyon, AZ, Grand Canyon Natural History Association, 1992

Hiking Tips - Hike Smart, accessed October 25, 2019, https://www.nps.gov/grca/planyourvisit/hike-tips.htm

History of the Train, accessed July 12, 2019, https://www.thetrain.com/the-train/history/

Hopi House, accessed October 11, 2019, http://grcahistory.org/sites/south-rim/hopi-house/

Kavanaugh, James, *Field Guide to the Grand Canyon: A folding Pocket Guide to Familiar Plants & Animals* (Pocket Naturalist Series), Safety Harbor, FL, Waterford Press, 2017

Layers in Time: Geology of Grand Canyon, accessed August 10, 2019, https://www.nps.gov/grca/learn/education/learning/upload/GeoArticle-11-1-11-2017.pdf

Leavengood, Betty, *Grand Canyon Women: Lives Shaped by Landscape*, Grand Canyon, AZ, Grand Canyon Association, 2004

Mary Colter's Buildings at Grand Canyon, accessed October 23, 2019, https://www.nps.gov/grca/learn/photosmultimedia/colter_index.htm

BIBLIOGRAPHY

Mary Colter's Lookout Studio, accessed October 15, 2019, https://www.nps.gov/grca/learn/photosmultimedia/colter_lookout_photos.htm

Mary Colter's Desert View Watchtower, accessed October 15, 2019, https://www.nps.gov/grca/learn/photosmultimedia/colter_index.htmhttps://www.nps.gov/grca/learn/photosmultimedia/mary-colter---indian-watchtower.htm

Mary Colter's Hopi House, accessed August 27, 2019, https://www.nps.gov/grca/learn/photosmultimedia/colter_hopih_photos.htm

Miller, Sara & Toole, Pat, *Path of the Thunderbird: A Grand Canyon Adventure*, Grand Canyon, AZ, Grand Canyon Association, 2017

Miners, accessed July 12, 2019, https://www.nps.gov/grca/learn/historyculture/miners.htm

Naming the Colorado River, July 5, 2017, accessed, January 17, 2020, https://www.mygrandcanyonpark.com/park/the-colorado-river

Yerian, Loretta, *Native American tribes captivate students with cultural traditions and storytelling*, February 17, 2015, accessed September 16, 2019, https://www.grandcanyonnews.com/news/2015/feb/17/native-american-tribes-captivate-students-with-cu/

One Day White Water Rafting, accessed July 5, 2019, https://grandcanyon.com/tours/south-rim-tours/one-day-whitewater-self-drive/

Park Statistics, accessed July 14, 2019, https://www.nps.gov/grca/learn/management/statistics.htm

Phantoms of the Past: A Historic Walking Tour, Grand Canyon, AZ, National Park Service, U.S. Department of the Interior

Phantom Ranch Junior Ranger, Grand Canyon, AZ, National Park Service, U.S. Department of the Interior

Places to Go, accessed August 5, 2019, https://www.nps.gov/grca/planyourvisit/placestogo.htm

Powell, J.W., The Exploration of the Colorado River and its Canyons, New York, NY, Dover Publications Inc., 1961

Preserving the Grand Canyon, January 2012, accessed January 21, 2020, https://www.theodorerooseveltcenter.org/Blog/Item/Preserving%20the%20Grand%20Canyon

South Rim Junior Ranger, Grand Canyon, AZ, National Park Service, U.S. Department of the Interior

Stanton, Robert Brewster, *Colorado River Controversies*, Boulder City, NE, Westwater Books, 1982

Suran, William C., *The Kolb Brothers of Grand Canyon*, Grand Canyon, AZ, Grand Canyon Natural History Association, 1991

Theodore Roosevelt makes Grand Canyon a national monument, accessed July 12, 2019, https://www.history.com/this-day-in-history/theodore-roosevelt-makes-grand-canyon-a-national-monument

Three leave Powell's Grand Canyon expedition, accessed January 17, 2020, https://www.history.com/this-day-in-history/three-leave-powells-grand-canyon-expedition

Thybony, Scott, *Phantom Ranch: Grand Canyon National Park*, Grand Canyon, AZ, Grand Canyon Association, 2001

Top 10 Things to Do with Kids in the Grand Canyon, accessed March 9, 2019, https://www.mygrandcanyonpark.com/things-to-do/kids-activities-grand-canyon

2 to 5 Day Noncommercial River Trips: Diamond Creek, accessed July 8, 2020, https://www. nps.gov/grca/planyourvisit/overview-diamond-ck.htm

Verkamp's Visitor Center, Assessed October 13, 2019, https://www.nps.gov/grca/planyourvisit/verkamps.htm

Your Perfect Week in the Grand Canyon, accessed March 9, 2019, https://www.mygrandcanyonpark.com/things-to-do/perfect-4-7-days

Non-Publication Sources

Backcountry Information Center, Grand Canyon National Park, AZ, March 2019

Bright Angel Campground, Grand Canyon National Park, AZ, March 2019

Bright Angel Lodge, Grand Canyon National Park, AZ, March 2019

Bright Angel Trail, Grand Canyon National Park, AZ, March 2019

Deitzer, Bill, Lecture, April 2019

Desert View Watch Tower, Grand Canyon National Park, AZ, March 2019

El Tovar Hotel, Grand Canyon National Park, AZ, March 2019

Grand Canyon Railway, Williams to Grand Canyon National Park, Williams, AZ, March 2019

Grand Canyon Visitor Center, Grand Canyon National Park, Grand Canyon, AZ, March 2019

Hauer, Kendall, Manuscript Review, Director, Limper Geology Museum, Miami University, Oxford, OH, January, 2020

Hopi House, Grand Canyon National Park, AZ, March 2019

Kaibab Trail, Grand Canyon National Park, AZ, March 2019

Kolb Studio, Grand Canyon National Park, AZ, March 2019

Lookout Studio, Grand Canyon National Park, AZ, March 2019

McClure, Edward M. (Ted), Manuscript Review, Librarian, Grand Canyon National Park Research Library, Grand Canyon National Park, AZ, December 2019

National Geographic Imax Movie, *Grand Canyon: The Hidden Secrets*, Tusayan, AZ, March 2019

National Park Ranger, Lecture, Tusayan Museum and Ruin, Grand Canyon National Park, AZ, March 2019

Phantom Ranch, Grand Canyon National Park, AZ, March 2019

Stoeberl, Todd, Lecture & e-mail correspondence, Acting Chief of Interpretation and Resource Education, Grand Canyon, AZ March, 2019 & December 2019

Sullivan, Eugenia (Jean), Manuscript Review, Librarian, Grand Canyon National Park Research Library, Grand Canyon National Park, AZ, December 2019

Tusayan Museum and Ruin, Grand Canyon National Park, AZ, March 2019

Verkamp's Visitor Center, Grand Canyon National Park, AZ, March 2019

Wilcox, Jennifer, Lecture & e-mail correspondence, Museum Administrator/ Educational Coordinator, National Cryptologic Museum, National Security Agency, February 2016 & January, 2016

Yavapai Geology Museum, Grand Canyon National Park, AZ, March 2019

ABOUT THE AUTHOR

Jeff Alt is an award-winning author, a talented speaker and a family hiking & camping expert. Alt has been hiking since his youth. In addition to writing the award-winning *Adventures of Bubba Jones* book series, Alt is the author three other award-winning books: *Four Boots-One Journey* (John Muir Trail), *Get Your Kids Hiking*, and *A Walk for Sunshine* (Appalachian Trail). *A Walk for Sunshine*. Alt is a member of the Outdoor Writers Association of America (OWAA) and the Society of Children's Book Writers and Illustrators (SCBWI). He has walked the Appalachian Trail, the John Muir Trail with his wife, and he carried his 21-month old daughter across a path of Ireland. Alt's son was on the Appalachian Trail at six weeks of age. Alt lives with his wife and two kids in Cincinnati, Ohio.

For more information about the Adventures of Bubba Jones visit: www.bubbajones.com

For more information about Jeff Alt visit: www.jeffalt.com

E-mail the author: jeff@jeffalt.com

MORE FROM THE BUBBA JONES SERIES

Great Smoky Mountains (2015)

Shenandoah National Park (2016)

Acadia National Park (2018)